Wilderness

A Collection of Dark Tales

ELIZABETH YON

"Farewell to the Flesh" was awarded First Place in Central PA Magazine's 2002 writing contest, and appeared the same year in the May issue of the magazine.

Cover Photo by Elizabeth Yon

ISBN: 1470191857
ISBN 13: 9781470191856

Table of Contents

Dear Reader

Welcome. I'm so pleased you could visit. See the forest ahead? That's where we're going. We'll have a bit of a ramble and look at some of the wildlife, but we won't touch. Oh my, no.

If you enjoy a little shiver now and then (and who doesn't), I think you'll find one or two here. Nothing too terrible – just keep your wits about you and don't go crashing off into the trees in panic. My woods are shadowy and vast, but if you stay on the path you'll probably be fine.

What might we see? Oh, ghosts and witches, werewolves, vampires, and workers of magic. They are a lively bunch and will come quite close to you (you may even feel a chill breath upon your neck), but it's all in good fun. You've most likely had some experience with such creatures, so I won't be concerned about leaving you to wander at your own pace.

Take care now, and enjoy the dark.

Snow Eva

⁂

The girl was born of the forest, cradled among the gnarled nooks of wild apple roots. She was silent and old looking, with eyes as glossily unyielding as apple seeds. Her little lips were fat and greedy, stained bloody as apple rind. Her skin was pale as apple flesh. A huntsman brought her to me in his pouch, dusted with the first snow of that portentous season. He might have kept or abandoned his strange find, but he knew his duty. I am the warden of this place, with a thousand eyes and ears.

"Place her on the board," I said, indicating the kitchen trestle. I was reluctant to touch her.

The huntsman gazed down at her. "My wife and I could care for her, my lady. She's only a wee bit. She'll need nursing."

"Do I not know how the young are raised? She will stay with me, she is my charge. Your wife may come here to nurse the child if her own brood can spare her."

His mouth trembled, but he did not dare defy me. "Aye, if that's the way of it," he said. He clutched the infant closer and added in a sulky voice, "The babe's not a foundling rabbit or fawn, you know."

He had formed an attachment to the child. It was as obvious as it was ridiculous, and I had no more patience for his intrusion on my solitude.

"Do not be impertinent. Put the child on the board and fetch your wife."

What a grim face he presented to me! He laid the baby on the trestle, tucking and fussing at the goatskin pouch. When he was satisfied with the infant's comfort, he fished in one of his many pockets and drew forth several wizened knobs of rueful red. He rolled them across the smooth waxed planks in distaste, as though they could infect him with some dire disease.

"Them's apples from the tree where I found her. I thought you might be wanting them for your studies."

The fruits were hard little scowls of tartness, the spiteful yield of a hoary forest hag long past bearing anything sweet. Their leathery skins rattled on the board. I touched one with the tip of my finger, and it was cold as death.

"You've done well," I told the huntsman. I pressed a coin into his hard palm, and sent him home.

The huntsman's wife was called Ilsa. She materialized out of that first unseasonable snow to scratch at the kitchen door, a lumpish assemblage of bosom and hips with a basket of bread and cheese over her arm. She smelled of milk and woman's blood, a warm fog of biological odor, over which lay a pungent top note of garlic and wood smoke.

"I'm come to nurse the babe, my lady," she said, staring at her feet.

"You'll find her just there. You may build up the fire."

I waved toward the wriggling bundle still on the kitchen board. I had not yet examined the child, but I had sliced and gutted the apples. Their petite, sour bodies housed seeds as black as grief. My reflection curved around them in a slippery puddle as I bent over them, trying to read their meaning in the grey November light.

The room was dim and cold, I suppose. I don't take notice of such things. Ilsa clucked and bustled, gathering the hungry infant to her breast while she worked. Soon, a great rush of flame ascended the chimney and the kettle swung to service. From under the loaves in the basket came herbs tied up in a rough muslin bundle: mint, chamomile, and lemony melissa. A tisane brewed and sent its sharp sweetness into the room on a heated cloud. I watched this industry from the opposite end of the board. Already, I felt overly warm.

Ilsa glanced up at me from under her lashes. "Please, my lady, what will you name the child?"

"Must she have a name? She is a wild creature. We do not name the deer or the fox." I could not recall my own name. Perhaps I hadn't one.

"But, my lady, the child is not an animal," cried the impudent woman.

"She is a product of the forest. What meaning she has, I do not know."

The forest has its ways, crooked as crow tracks. Its spiraling embroideries collapse upon and regenerate themselves, the spirit board of the gods who never tire of trying to be heard. I was uneasy over the interpretation of the child, such a strange and ill-omened babe, and over the interpretation of the ancient apple's final fruiting – for I was certain that it was final. The early November snow had fallen on both like a finger of light, pointing to their significance.

I took down from a shelf my mortar and pestle and regarded the apple seeds. The trees of the village orchards are pampered grafts of cultivated hybrids upon the accommodating rootstock of the wild apple. One cannot grow these chimeras from the seeds of their fruit, for they will only revert to their wild origin. Their deeper truth will out. I ruminated on the answers inherent in the seeds before me. I planted one ebon pip in the kitchen herb pot. Five more I crushed, and bottled the bitter powder.

"My lady?"

I looked up from my work, surprised to find the huntsman's wife still seated by the fire with the babe at one great white teat, awaiting an answer to her absurd question.

"Hmm? Ilsa, you irritate me. Be silent. Call the creature whatever you like."

And so the girl came to be known as Snow Eva.

I have no children of my own, nor do I recall my parents or siblings. Yet mine is surely an ancient family. The proof of it is all about me in the mossy stones and towers of this house, much broken and tumbled now, and in the forest that creeps for miles away from the heavy walls. I remember the forest from long before my birth, and my place in it that is my true inheritance. It is my only book, and though it is a great hardship to read it, the answers to every question are there writ. The laws of the forest are the laws of all existence, and the first of these is patience.

Snow Eva was a chapter of more than ordinary complexity. The babe thrived, as I knew she would, for she was a message of terrible import. For five years I watched her grow, and as she grew so grew the apple seedling in its rough clay pot until the tree had to be set in the ruin of the garden, to spread its blind greedy roots in the feral soil. The child was solemn, pale of face, with hair like moonless night. The tree was equally pale, its slender stalk like a naked bone, and its leaves were blackest green. I looked upon the girl with dread, feeling the weight of time passing, and with a painful longing. Love was like a stone in my heart, and I longed to tear it out.

Finally, I took her into the forest and showed her the ragged remains of the ancient apple that had birthed her. The tree stood near a deep black pool, the white and twisted trunk cracked and fallen away. I thought it looked uncannily like one of the long-broken towers of my house. No life resided in the beetle-eaten corpse of the old apple, but I saw that a seedling had sprung up from among its sheltering roots and had grown tall and strong, thrusting its progenitor aside and even supping on its decay.

I grasped Snow Eva by her meager arm and dragged her to the tree. The girl was slow and stumbling from our long walk, and I lightly slapped her face to command her attention.

"Never eat of this fruit, for it is your kin," I said. I gave her a little shake. "To offend the tree in such a way means death. Repeat what I have told you."

If nothing else, she had learned attentiveness in my care. She repeated her lesson in a grave, lisping voice, and I was satisfied.

"You may have your supper," I told her, and handed her the pack from my back.

The day had grown late, so laborious had been my progress with the child dragging at my heels. I watched her take a cold meat pie from the pack and squat in the lank grass with it, nibbling like a mouse. She was not strong, but rather tenacious. Again, I thought of my ruined towers, and the slender vines that had pried at the stones until they toppled.

Another year traversed the great circle of the seasons, and then another. Between my studies and my duties, I was often gone into the forest for days at a time. When I returned, Snow Eva would run to me and comb the brambles and snarls from my hair.

"Auntie, why do you go away into the woods," she asked one day as she performed this charming act of grooming.

The question discomfited me. I have never been ashamed of my ways, for they are what make it possible for me to ward this place and, in any case, I cannot change my nature. Still, I would not discuss such things with a child. I offered only a brusque explanation.

"I must run across the miles and see that all is well in the forest. It is my charge, as it has been that of my family for long ages."

I looked into the big liquid eyes and saw tears welling up. The girl wept more often than I would have thought possible, and certainly more than was practical, though her tears were always quietly shed.

To forestall them, I said, "If you are lonely in my absence I cannot help it. You are safe here, as you well know."

She sniffled. "Am I of your family?"

Well, was she? I did not know, and though my traitorous heart gave a leap at the thought, my brain had a colder response. All my long life, I have been the only warden. I was silent as Snow Eva brought the basin for me to wash my blackened feet. I thought to shift the conversation to safer ground.

"Look outside the kitchen door, my girl. The huntsman has brought us a small doe for our larder. What do you think of venison stew?"

"Oh, that wasn't the huntsman brought the doe," said the cheeky girl. "I saw you put it there yourself. Did you kill it?"

"Yes," I huffed, put out at being discovered in a lie. It is an evil habit.

"Auntie, how is it you are able to run so far and so fast? How is it you can see all that happens in the forest?"

I started up with growl. Snow Eva stepped back, but thrust out her chin in a defiant attitude. Tick, tick, tick went the red clock in my brain, and I shrugged inside my skin that felt new and tight. The moment passed.

"Go and do your chores," I said.

But I did not forget the challenge. No. Sadly, I could not.

I dressed the doe myself and set a portion of it to roast. Snow Eva chopped vegetables, standing at the board on an upturned crate. We did not speak, each lost in her own thoughts, though we cast sidelong glances at one another. For my own part, I saw that I was at fault. For too long I had neglected the question of the girl's meaning. I went to the kitchen window and looked out on the apple tree. The moon rose behind it, round and smooth, and stared through the black leaves at me with blank indifference. It is a cruel mistress and knows only the language of blood and small cries in the night. Its cold, white face filled me suddenly with a desire to see my own.

It had been long since I had seen my reflection with any clarity, though I had often read my bones with my fingertips. The strong line of jaw, the hollows and curves of cheek and forehead, were both familiar and cryptic. The forest knows nothing of the art of glass gazing, nor cares for the alluring reversal of the mirrored world. Thus, I owned but one looking-glass — a darkened relic that stood beneath a moth-eaten drapery in a moldering bedchamber in a ruined section of the house. I turned to the girl, who was scraping the chopped onions and parsnips into the stew pot.

"I am going along the east corridor," I said. "I will be back shortly, see to the supper."

Snow Eva regarded me with ill-concealed curiosity. "May I go, too?"

She had never been through the dark warren of ancient corridors; we lived quite comfortably in the two rooms that adjoined the kitchen. The house was treacherous in its decrepitude, and easy to become lost in.

"No," I said. I pointed across the garden, which forms a sort of courtyard at the center of the house. "See that window, just behind the apple tree, the one with the broken panes in the upper half? I will be there."

"I will fetch you a lamp." She went to the sideboard and trimmed the wick.

I took it from her, and went to the heavy oaken door that led to the east corridor. It groaned like a dying man when I pulled it by its iron ring, and thick shrouds of cobweb came loose from the wall with a sound like ripping silk. I closed it behind me, and set off into the musty darkness. My lamp was soon snuffed out by the dank gusts of air that fluttered along the echoing halls. I set it on a heap of tumbled stone and went on without it. I hadn't needed it to see, anyway.

The house had slumped further into rot than I had realized. It had been many long years since I had troubled to walk this way. The dust had been thick upon the floors even then, and the prints of my earlier passage were preserved as in a tomb. They, too, led to the bedchamber with the mirror in it, and I recalled my last sight of my reflected face and form. I had returned from my patrol of the forest and gone straight to the looking-glass. I had gone swiftly, with my brain already shifting back to thoughts of my studies and with my skin itching and shrinking. I had time for only a glimpse of my other self — the strong, lean form of the warden. I will never forget its beauty.

Now, I stepped to the mirror and stripped off the drapery. It fell to dust in my hand. The glass was much spotted with black blooms where the silver had worn from its back, and the ornate frame was cracked and blistered. With my sleeve, I wiped away the film left by the rotting drapery. The fat moon glided into the window frame and poured its stark light upon me. I let drop my gown. I was thin and ropy with muscle, my ribs embossed upon my skin. My face was narrow, long jawed and hollow. My eyes were the silvery-grey of river ice, and I saw that they now gleamed forth from a starburst of fine lines. I was surprised to see threads of silver in the shadow color of my hair.

In the glass with me, intruding upon and almost pushing aside my reflection, was the image of the wild apple tree I had grown in my garden. It was lithe and vigorous, reaching upward with young white arms. It shook down its lush dark foliage like hair in the night breeze. Its sinewy claws grasped at the moon, defiant and curious. Seeing this, I finally understood the answer to a seven-year-old riddle. My way was clear. Before I left the bedchamber, I smashed the mirror that had helped me to see it.

When I was younger than Snow Eva, the forest taught me this lesson: transformation is the abnegation of death. And so the forest transforms itself season to season and renounces its right to oblivion, as do its denizens who desire only life. It produces many possibilities in its shape shifting zeal, many possibilities.

I meditated on this as I mixed the long-saved powdered apple seeds into the supper stew. It is the forest law that the strong should prevail over the weak, that threat should be met with savage force, and that there should be one warden over it all.

The girl busied herself with sweeping the hearth as I filled our bowls.

"Come and eat," I said, and if my heart cried out or if my hand trembled as I set the stew before her, my brain only repeated the law of the forest.

No Rest For The Wicked

﹏﹏﹏

Along about noon, when the shadows are stretched out straight and stiff as the dead, the Devil takes his daily constitutional about town. Part pleasure, part business, he observes the townsfolk during the languid hour when the sunshine lies hot and brittle over the neighborhoods like a hard candy glaze and folks are inclined to take themselves a little rest. The Devil does not rest, though. At the first booming stroke of the courthouse clock, he leaves his big old house in the historic district and strolls down his tree-lined block – in sun, then in shade – walking unscathed along the knife-edged boundary between light and dark, to the town center. His white summer suit is pristine and crisp despite the mugginess, his gait is leisurely, and his eyes pinwheel in their deep sockets as they take in everything along his route. He enjoys the spectacle of his neighbors and the quiet, if stifling, beauty of the day. But he always keeps an eye open for work undone, for his daily perambulations are also hunts.

The Devil can see old man Marchand asleep on his porch, lulled by the motion of his rocking chair and the cooling effect of his third mint julep. Even from the glare of the sidewalk, the glowing, vertiginous eyes can see each bead of condensation on the tall glass and mark their slow liquid slide until they drop, one by one, to the spreading dampness on Mr. Marchand's thigh. The Devil has lived two houses down from the Marchands for some time, and never fails to send Mr. Marchand a bottle of his favorite whiskey at the holidays, or to invite him over for a drink or two several times a week. This social calling has become easier, and far more pleasant, in the last year since Mrs. Marchand left.

Walking along in his relaxed swinging stride, the Devil can see, in the house on the corner, the Oldman twins asleep on their mama's bed under the big ceiling fan. They lie facing one another, their dark hair curling damply along their brows, their knees touching. He has watched them grow for ten years, has given them candy and quarters, has observed that though they are identical in their looks, they are very different in the privacy of their minds. He can see how the fan's paddles whicker through the light in the room, stirring it like a witch's brew, and he can see the red dream one twin dreams about the other. Shaking his head in avuncular fashion, the Devil strolls on. Boys will be boys, and little Patrick will soon be the only boy in the Oldman household.

Crossing into the newly refurbished arts district, where the squalid old row houses have been bought by young up-and-comers with money and energy to make them princely again, the Devil casts an eye toward Number 6 Robesham Place. It is the home of the Henrys, bright with fresh paint and fresh with bright flowers nodding from the hayrack planter on the stoop rail. Through the oval glass of the front door, he can see a glittering ice sculpture of a chandelier hanging in the foyer. He can see Mrs. Henry, upstairs in her shuttered bedroom, turn from her mirror, graceful as a music box dancer, and lift her thin chemise over her head. He can see how her white breasts stretch upward, the nipples an aching invitation to Mr. Lester Aubrey who sits on the edge of her bed, naked as a newborn babe. Mr. Aubrey's brushes and paints lie in the corner, still in his workbox, and the canvas on the easel by the window is dark and blank. The Devil chuckles. This is a two-for-the-price-of-one situation. In fact, it may be even better than that, since Mrs. Henry's is not the only lady's portrait on which Mr. Aubrey is woefully behind. He is incorrigible!

The Devil has come at last to the business district, very close to his destination. In a lovely old brick house that has been converted to real estate offices, he can see Mr. Henry reclining in noontime slump, feet on his desk, smoking. The Devil thinks to join him, removes a slim cigar from his breast pocket, and bites the end cleanly off with his strong white teeth. As he puts it between his lips, an aromatic smoke curls up from its tip and hangs in the still, fragile air like a ghostly skull. Mr. Henry is the dark horse in the Henry-Aubrey equation. The Devil can see that Mr. Henry's nerves are taut, that knowledge like a cold serpent has wound into the black passageways of Mr. Henry's thoughts. There is a revolver in the right hand desk drawer, well-oiled and loaded with grief. Even the Devil cannot predict what use Mr. Henry may make of it, and the uncertainty, the anticipation, is delicious.

The Devil has traversed several blocks and looked upon the silent carnival of grim wonders the town has to display, and yet the wicked-edged shadows have not moved. The sonorous voice of the courthouse clock still calls the noon hour. Precisely on the last stroke, the Devil arrives at the white frame church on the town square. In the midday glare, the church burns like a star. Its stained glass windows are kaleidoscopic fever dreams. The Devil looks beyond its scarlet doors to the dim rows of oaken pews and sees a woman, grey and stooped. She is rubbing beeswax polish into the age-darkened wood, burnishing it with a flannel rag as her lips move in prayer, or song, or simple conversation. Her children are long dead, her husband just set into the earth the week past. She has always been unassailable, but she is alone now. She is the prey, and this is, after all, a hunt. The Devil sighs, squares his shoulders, drops his cigar to the clean pavement, and enters the church.

A Solstice Riddle

※※※

I t was midsummer morning, blue and clear, with the first hint of the sun's heat rising from the grass into the brilliant air, when the plane fell on Lydia Greenway's house. It was the hour of herbal contemplation for Lydia, the aromatic denizens of her garden now being dry of the early dew and releasing their volatile oils to the touch of the sun. Lydia stepped through a riot of mint, sage, and lavender with the precise, floating delicacy of a ballerina. Her house sat at the edge of a neat rectangular hay field, and the warming air teased the clean spice from the hay. Lydia breathed it in with the earthy perfume of her herbs.

She could hear the athletic drone of the little plane as it swooped and waggled against the blue, the pilot enjoying a frisky morning of stunts. Most irritating! The fragile magic of the solstice was cracked, the birds fell silent, and the sleepy conversation of the bees was rendered inaudible. Lydia's nose quivered, an instrument of superlative accuracy, and she thought she could detect a nauseating reek of fuel and mechanical brio from the plane high above her. That this fleeting moment of perfect abundant light, this momentous turn of the great seasonal wheel, should be fractured and desecrated by the idiot now shredding the lazy clouds was insupportable. Lydia's brows drew together in stormy maleficence.

Simultaneously, it was the appointed hour for the start of the village church's picnic brunch, *Summer Celebration!,* and the long plank tables were draped with pristine cloths and laden with mushroom quiches and strawberry trifles. The Vacation Bible School students whooped and galloped and rolled on the grass, released from the musty church basement but carefully segregated from the staid pleasures of brunch preparation, and generally subjected one another to the unbridled savagery of play. As the final platters and bowls were set upon the tables, the pastor and his hungry congregation sat down to the highly anticipated meal and tucked their napkins beneath their chins. The Amen had resounded and forks were lifted when the little plane that had been entertaining the children with its aerial acrobatics emitted an embarrassed cough. All eyes rose to the heavens.

The plane was lower, and a gay streamer of smoke trailed it as it buzzed the treetops, heading for the village and the *Summer Celebration!* participants. The organist uttered a breathy shriek and several parishioners dropped their utensils and dove beneath the flapping tablecloths. Pastor Clume, mistaking the pilot's desperate dive for another more thrilling stunt, happily waved his napkin as the plane roared by, sucking his wispy hair vertical. The pilot pulled on the stick and managed a wobbling loop that took him above the humble rooftops, and then headed for the only open ground he could spy.

The plane bucked in the air, low enough now to cut a swath across the tops of the tall grasses; their green-gold heads whickered and snapped against the speeding fuselage. The pilot was at first relieved to think he had managed a safe landing, but he was coming in fast and suddenly there was a house before him. Again the mighty heave upon the stick, his eyes starting from their sockets. The plane screamed and tried to rise, belched explosively, hung like an ominous cloud for the barest second, and then fell like Lucifer on the house of the village witch.

Pastor Clume and the picnickers stampeded to the scene - wailing women in floating summer chiffon, red-faced men in white loafers and pastel suspenders, strawberry-kissed napkins still waving from several shirt fronts. The children, with the unsympathetic curiosity of youth, craned their necks from a distance deemed safe by the Bible School monitors, hoping to see Lydia's feet sticking out from the wreckage like the witch in The Wizard of Oz. They were disappointed to find that the house, though a bit squashed on the western side, still stood sturdily inside its white picket fence, the fabled herb garden untouched by the catastrophe. There were no flames or detonations, no bloody corpses were evident, and the pilot climbed from the burst pod of his plane wearing the shocked expression of a freshly slapped newborn.

"Praise the Lord," shouted Pastor Clume. Turning to the younger men in the gaggle, he snapped into emergency mode. "Tom, Harvey, help that man down. Mike, go get Doc Havers. Bob, let's find Miss Lydia. Ladies, please take those children home or back to the church. Thank you."

The pastor, not seen as a man of action in the normal course of events, was obeyed without question. His respectable paunch and myopic downy chick facade hid a clear-thinking paragon of military precision. Rolling up his sleeves, Clume prepared to enter the wounded house. This was not how he had envisioned his first entry to the home of Miss Lydia Greenway. Clattering across the shady porch, he experienced a sheepish pang of regret as he recalled how season after season had melted into years during which he had made only the most superficial assaults upon the woman's determined avoidance of his church. On one memorable late spring evening, he had strolled past her front garden no less than three times, priming his nerve and trying to get a discreet glimpse in the windows. The house had been utterly still, towering out of the gorgeous tangle of its undisciplined garden like a castle in a fairy tale.

The garden had not been still, Pastor Clume remembered with a thrill of unease. The roses grappling the front arbor were red as spilled blood and vital in a way that made him wary of entering the gate. To pass beneath them, to travel through that dark tunnel in the embrace of their wickedly thorn-spangled tentacles, required a heroic effort of will. Something had rustled overhead in the night-green foliage, and he had skipped through as though stung, emerging into a whispering world of rampant plant life and small scurryings. The stone walkway curved ahead of him through the heart of the garden, and the house that had seemed to loom over the street now appeared to have picked up its skirts and danced out of reach. It beckoned from the distance, and the garden flexed and shrugged in readiness to receive him.

An enormous bed of peonies, fleshily lush as Rubens's women, released their spicy sweet sighs as he brushed past, and he felt red heat mount into his face. He mopped it with his handkerchief and reproached himself as fanciful. The ruffled, bearded faces of the irises leaned toward him, grinning, their satyrs' jaws dripping. Carpets of thyme crept out to make him stumble; clematis blossoms descended on tender green threads to brush his cheek with moth-wing petals, bulwarks of lemon balm impeded him. He reeled around a curve in the path, half-drunk with twilight and disturbing thoughts, and saw a tall, slim hare sitting in an expanse of silver-green sage and violently pink dianthus. The creature was smoke-colored and gaunt as a greyhound with little red eyes that fastened on him in frank appraisal. Its eyes were incarnadine wells of infinite perception into which Pastor Clume felt himself slipping, rends in the fabric of the everyday through which he could plummet and fall forever as the red perusal stripped him of every secret, down to the unconscious workings of his individual cells.

"Well, well, Pastor Clume. What brings you to my garden?"

The voice was rough and low, worked upon by the rasp of decades of cigarettes. Indeed, the glowing red tip of Lydia's hand rolled smoke winked out at him from the deep gloom of the vine-enveloped porch, the suffocating sweet of honeysuckle mingling with the scent of burning cloves. The beastly hare was gone, and Clume's senses were overloaded and a-tremble as they had not been since his wild college days. The pastor heaved a restorative gulp of night air (*when had it become so dark?*) and pasted a smile onto his dazed face. From the dubious safety of the garden path, he proffered his invitation to Sunday service with the ardent eloquence of a suitor.

He had never returned to Lydia Greenway's house after that night, and had found perfectly acceptable reasons to duck into the hardware store or into the café when faced with passing her on the street. If his afternoon routine took him to the post office a quarter of an hour later than Lydia's took her, it was mere coincidence, and he peered out the front window of the parsonage first only to ascertain the need for an umbrella. He was not a superstitious man, and he scoffed at the village rumors (seeded about, he suspected, by some rather naughty boys) that Miss Lydia was a witch. He could not encourage such childish talk, and cautioned his congregation most sternly against it.

Now, as Bob pushed open the tall front door and bellowed for Lydia, Pastor Clume felt a distinct reluctance to enter warring in his breast with his natural desire to tender aid. The men stumbled over one another in the narrow hallway, and pressed forward into the front parlor where they stopped in confusion. The room was bare of furniture. There were no pictures on the walls, no rugs on the floor - only the heavy damask drapes hinted at occupation. There was no film of dust or festooning cobweb to speak of neglect. The parlor was empty and waiting as a stage. They moved as one into the dining room, no longer shouting for Miss Lydia, subdued by strangeness.

"Here, what's going on?" Bob cast a suspicious eye around the equally empty and echoing dining room. "She can't have moved her things out with no one seein' her."

Pastor Clume felt the air had become very thin. "Maybe she uses only the upstairs part of the house?"

They stumped up the stair and poked into each of the three bedrooms. Nothing. The bathroom was pristine and cold as a tomb, with no towels or soaps laid out. They tramped up to the attic. It was bereft of the boxes and trunks typical to such a space, and like the rest of the house was swept scrupulously clean. Descending to the kitchen, they found a room equipped with appliances that were not plugged in, cupboards that were bare, and a light fixture with no bulbs in it. The damage from the fallen plane was worst here, and plaster and lathe lay strewn about in a billow of white dust. Written on this snowy surface were glyphs of passage unmistakable as anything but the footprints of a hare.

Farewell To The Flesh

H aunts are common enough, here in the Big Easy. They hang in the greasy shadows, disguised by the curvaceous silhouettes of the iron balconies. When a girl stumbles out from the hot, smoky night places into the humid arms of the dark, there are haunts enough if she's sense to see them.

I'm a night trader. Ain't got no use for all that Southern sunlight everybody always flying down here to soak up. Me, I'm like a bayou gator. I cruise out on a ribbon of moonlight, hunting for a good meal, a little loving. I sing in the night like them gators do. I call in my lovers, and wicked haunts cling to them like wet silk. My lovers don't know no better. I help them a little beyond what they expecting, and they pay me just the same.

I read tea leaves, cards, maybe some knucklebones, sitting on a red velvet cushion in the narrow front parlor of Madame Lele's. Right next door, they serve up red beans and rice with hot sauce so fiery it smokes, and the juke just about busts through the thin wall between us, it's so damn loud. That place, it serves liquor, too. My customers stagger in on the fumes and beg for good fortunes in whiskey-burned voices. They don't know the hungry dead ride around on their backs, playing tricks. I read for them, then I take them through the beaded curtain and ease them on down on that big old purple fainting couch Madame got from a burned-out plantation house. When I touch the men, they quiver. They afraid of the mojo thickening the air. The women only sigh and open their arms. My sisters are practical. I'm compassionate when I kiss their whiskey lips.

Madame's got a old juju gator head hanging in there. It stares down while I make shadows on the wall with my lovers. All the inky knots and tendrils look awful pretty, and the haunts get confused, caught in that black web. When my lovers faint from the ecstasy, as often happens, I reach out and run my fingers over those shadows gathering the whole tangle into a little ball. I pinch it hard. Inside is a nasty haunt, struggling to free itself. I take that little ball, and I offer it to Old Gator Head, there on the wall. He grins just like he still in the bayou with all his kin. I hold that ball under his toothy snout, and *snap!* Down it goes, haunt and all. I never figured out where he puts them, seeing as how he's got no stomach no more. But Madame's juju is a mighty powerful one.

That gator, he's got hisself some expensive glass eyeballs, real as life. Liquid gold flecks floating over deep amber. They stir a memory in me of the swamp, the way it lies all quiet with the sunshine stepping over the green-gold floating lace. But underneath, the water's dark as tea, with big jaws hiding in the murk. Mr. Gator's eyes make me feel like he's sizing me up for a meal. Sometimes, from the corner of my own eye, I think I see that juju head wink in a slow gator way. The filmy secret eyelid slides up over that cold glitter like fog rolling over the swamp. Times like that, I get the hot, ripe smell of the mud and moss in my nose sure as if I was standing in it, and I think of the sound bones make breaking.

Madame's got another girl works in the parlor, too. She calls her Jolie, as in *jolie laide*, on account of Jolie's popular with the men even though she's got a big nose and a flat chest. When it comes to fortunetelling, Jolie's a stone fraud. She makes up any crazy story for the customers, long as it makes 'em smile. She got no talent for divining. It's a different story when it comes to the fainting couch, though. Jolie does it for extra cash, and she's afraid of the juju. Not like me. I never charge for ridding a customer of haunts. When Jolie takes a body back behind the beaded curtain, she throws a black Spanish lace shawl over Old Gator Head. Says it creeps her to have him staring down on her. She never sees the haunts, either. Dumb as a post is our Jolie, but she got a good heart.

Madame swept in at 10 o'clock like she does every evening, just to check on the business. She pretends she don't know about what goes on in the room with the fainting couch, but I think she's wise. Madame's a big woman, all bosom and rolling hips under a caftan the size of a revival tent. She crops her hair tight to her scalp and dyes it blond. It stands out against her dark skin like the white tip of a match. She smells like fresh-baked bread and orange oil.

"Lord!" she sang, just like she at choir practice. "Look at the dust! Jolie, honey, get the broom." She whisked away the Spanish shawl from the juju head and frowned. "Baby, don't be covering up the gator. Can't do his job proper if he can't see."

"Yes, ma'am," Jolie mumbled, and scuffed at the linoleum with the balding broom.

Madame stared at me, where I sat in the darkened corner on a footstool. She's got a big aura of light around her like she swallowed the sun, and no haunts ever ride her shoulders. She stared like she going to say something to me, then pursed her lips and turned away with a *harrumph*.

"Jolie, you been conjuring the dead in here?" Madame wrinkled her nose. "Smells like the swamp. You know I don't hold with any of that Devil's work. You stick to the cards, girl, and you be all right."

Jolie sighed, and dropped the broom into my corner with a smirk. "Probably that smelly ol' gator stinking up the place," she whispered.

The Professor came to the parlor a few days before Mardi Gras. I seen him standing out in the neon gaudy street, looking at our flickering sign shaped like a hand with a spiral in the palm. He had his lip all curled, and a mean glint in his eye. I felt a faintness come over me, watching him stroll real casual up to the door, and I went in the back and wouldn't read for him. Jolie flounced down on the red cushion, got her long legs all screwed up into a knot, and made herself mysterious. She got a husky voice the men like, and the Professor wasn't no different. He liked her bare shoulders in her little strappy dress, too. Pretty soon, Jolie was leading him back behind the curtain, and I hid in the bathroom. The Professor taught classes on local superstitions and the history of voodoo. He laughed at the gator head, and wouldn't let Jolie cover it up like she wanted.

"Ah, chere, let him watch if that's what he likes."

He shoved her down rough and bruised her good before he was through. I shivered behind the bathroom door, listening to her whimper. I was too scared to go out there, because the Professor had the most devilish haunt riding him I'd ever seen. It was a shadowy halo all around him. While he took what he wanted from poor Jolie, it went creeping out like the fingers of a huge hand, sucking up the lamplight and popping bulbs. Later, Jolie stood crying in front of the bath-room mirror. She had long, red welts down her back to her pale, skinny thighs.

"Look what that sonofabitch done," she raged. She flung down the wad of bills she had clenched in her fist. "Got his thrills cheap, too!"

The Professor came back three times. First, Jolie locked him out and threatened to call the police. He snarled and called her a whore, and I began to remember. The next time he came, he put his shoulder to the door, and the lock burst just like it did the night he came to my apartment. I had dropped his class by then, but it was too, too late.

Jolie ran like a streak of lightning out the back, through the narrow alley and into the juke joint next door. The Professor stood in Madame Lele's parlor and sniffed for Jolie's perfume. I stayed in the shadowy corner of the back room where the light couldn't reach, and watched him knock over the reading table.

The hanging lamp, with its dim bulb, swung like laundry in a gale. Above my head, the gator showed his teeth and growled. I wasn't scared anymore. I remembered what the Professor had done, and why I was there.

The last time the Professor came, I let him into the tiny parlor. Lord, was he surprised. The din of Mardi Gras was loose in the city, folks in masks and costumes staggering between shadows and light all through the Vieux Carre. Carnival. The last farewell to the flesh before penitence.

I smiled at the Professor with all my teeth. I pulled him toward the purple couch the way I would a lover. I pushed him down on the velvet gently, so gently.

He was triumphant. "I knew you'd come around, chere. There was never any need for games."

Mean lust smoldered in him, and the haunt that rode him billowed up like smoke, big and black. I knew it was no ghost, no dead thing refusing to pass. It came from inside the Professor, projected like the movies in the theater. I made shadows with him on the wall, and the haunt wound itself into the dark filigree the way the big snakes wind up into the trees in the swamp. The Professor's blood heated. Our skin steamed like the thick clinging mud. The smells of sex and bayou mingled. The Professor fell back, exhausted. I passed my hand over the tangled skein of shadow on the wall. Gathering. Gathering. He watched me from lazy eyes as I showed him the inky ball pinched between my fingers, its slender tail tethered to his heart.

"What's that, chere?"

I smiled down at him. Jolie's knees gripped his ribs hard as I sat on his abdomen.

"This is what you owe me, Professor. This is the payment for crushed limbs and lungs filled with swamp water. Payment for my bones, in the belly of a gator."

I showed him my true face, Jolie's cheekbones broadening, her eyes tilting up, her lips swelling into full ruby petals, skin darkening to café au lait. He screamed and thrashed under Jolie's strong thighs. He screamed when the gator closed its jaws on the little ball of shadow. He screamed until the fine, dark thread of his soul snapped.

𝔄utumn 𝔏andscape

⚜

The woman with the red hair stood alone in the art museum gallery. Before her was a vast canvas in three vivid colors – blue, green, and white. It was a simple piece like a child's puzzle, the expanses of blue and green empty yet inviting the eye to rest in their coolness. The woman thought they seemed like a grassy hill under an autumn sky. And though it was not in evidence in the painting, she felt the sun was there, filling the canvas with light. The smaller white object gave the impression of motion. The woman could not have said how it moved, or by what magic brushstroke the artist conveyed the sense of it, but she found it bobbing and ghosting gaily in the periphery of her vision again and again, only to become a fixed splotch of titanium white when she looked directly at it. Disturbed, she moved on through the dim, echoing galleries where the late afternoon shadows spilled from the vaults and pillars and pooled on the buff terrazzo tiles.

The next day, in the blind, obliterating glare of noon, the woman returned to the small gallery. Again, she was the only observer of the tri-color painting. She looked into the green and blue landscape - for bare of trees or gardens as it was, she felt it *was* a landscape - and thought she discerned a slight breeze sliding over the round shoulder of the hill. Yes, a breath, a sigh of crisp autumnal air touched her cheek and stirred the tendrils of her hair. She could smell the green, a cold crush of meadow ruffled by the breeze, sweet and sad in best October form. The little white object, really no more than a splash from a loaded brush, seemed to caper on the hillside. It was bolder today, dancing before her astonished eyes and subtly reshaping itself. A docent peeked into the gallery, smiled, and went away on rubber-soled feet. The white object was once again just a splash of paint.

On the third day in the empty gallery, the woman made a decision. She would touch the painting, the most forbidden of acts, to see what it felt like beneath her fingers. Standing in front of the canvas, she looked down at her feet where the toes of her conservative pumps nudged the decorative line of Greek key tiles that marked the boundary between the art and the viewer. The museum was trusting of its patrons, and felt that a rail or a rope was impolite. It had never had cause to regret that trust. The gallery was mute and sleepy, forgotten at the end of the wide corridor that opened onto other, more popular, rooms. In one swift movement, the woman stepped forward and laid her palm against the canvas, against the ridges and hollows of the impasto, and felt...soft, susurrus grass.

The white thing on the hill was a horse. Why hadn't she seen that before? The little horse leaped and shimmied, tossing its head and rolling its eyes at her. It was tethered there, and pulled at its binding with bouncy energy. The woman became afraid it would it harm itself and her concern propelled her forward, through the interface of gallery air and painted surface, onto the grassy hill. The cool grass tickled her ankles as she walked to the horse and held out her hand. The creature was not only white, but had swirls of pewter and pearl dappling its hide. Its belly held a bluish shadow, and its mane and tail foamed upon the breeze. It ceased its bounding and pranced in place as she crept forward and slipped the grey halter from its head. Its short, smooth fur was cool and damp like mist, the softest tactile experience she had ever known. As the halter fell to the green crown of the hill, a wind charged up its gentle slope and blew her skirt skyward. The woman gasped and slapped it down with both hands and —

-stood looking at the painting of greenbluewhite on the wall of the silent forgotten gallery. Its rough texture suggested more than ever a hillside and a soaring blue autumn sky. The effect was magnified by a frisking cloud in many shades of white and grey.

Beauty & The Eye
Of The Beholder

M artha was an unhappy girl approaching the towering opportunity
of her senior prom. She hadn't, of course, been asked to attend as
anyone's date, but she was going anyway. Prom, in Martha's opinion,
constituted a defining moment in a person's life, especially in a girl's life, and
she meant to have the best memory of that moment she could manufacture.
Her determination was grim. She approached the problem of prom night like
a general ordering troops for battle. Martha was not convinced of the merits
of either spontaneity or serendipity. She was not a believer in romantic magic.
Prom was a prize to be won through hard labor.

Scrutinizing her reflection, Martha started her preparations with a list.
First, her hair would be cut, colored and styled. The hair she saw was shoulder
length, thick, and walnut brown with glossy swoops of natural wave. Lovely
hair. Martha didn't think so. To her, it was a mousy nest abandoned by some
furtive animal, lacking form, vibrancy, and the mysterious shining tactile invitation she discerned in the hair of her classmates. It wouldn't do, and it would
be fixed.

Next, her makeup would be applied at a salon, and her fingers and toes tipped with pearly pink. Martha's face was fresh and open, with clear grey eyes and rosy lips that were ready to smile, if only she would let them. Just now, they were frowning in concentration. Martha despaired of ever achieving the pouty, high-cheekboned look of the models in her fashion magazines. Her face, she thought, was too round and plain. She fervently hoped the cosmetologist at the salon could draw a new one.

Finally, there was the enormous challenge of the dress. Martha scanned her body head to toe, turned sideways to take stock of her thickness, revolved and attempted with the aid of a hand mirror to assess her rear view. Her form was petite and athletic, pleasing womanly curves were surfacing, and her limbs were strong and straight. Martha was disgusted. She observed bulges where she felt there should be smoothness, too much of her everywhere when the slimness of a knife edge was the vogue, and no height to speak of. Her dress would be called on to rectify these deformities, and therefore could be of no ordinary make. She had saved for two years from her babysitting money, and she meant to shoot the works on a gown of such fabulousness only one woman could possibly create it.

Madame Babatskaya, at ease in the frilly chaos of her dress shop as a spider in the center of her web, poured tea for her seventeen-year-old visitor. The old woman was wrinkled as a tortoise, her obviously dyed mass of boot black hair piled atop her head in the style of an empress. Her face, that had been beautiful in her youth, was painted in the high, hectic color of a theater poster, and huge flashing gems weighted her pendulous earlobes and gnarled claws. Madame carried herself with regal assurance, and never blushed to flirt with young men a third her age. Her confidence rather shocked Martha, who was busily describing the éclat with which she wanted to amaze her fellow prom-goers.

Madame, sipping tea and watching the feverish color leap in Martha's face, interrupted the girl's monologue. "Martha is such a pretty name, so unusual these days."

Martha stuttered to a halt. She hated her name. All her classmates had cute names like Tiffani, and Brittney, and Courtney. Martha was named for her grandmother, who had owned a bakery and been famous for her operatic contralto, exercised while she kneaded bread dough. Martha remembered her as a big woman with brawny arms and red knuckles the size of shooter marbles. She closed her eyes and a tear slipped out. Madame effected not to notice.

"You are a lovely gurrrl," she said, spinning the word out with a purr. "Such skin! Such eyes! You will break many hearts. I can make your gown, but a gown is only wrapping. You want more?"

"Yes," Martha whispered in the depths of her misery. "I want more. I want to be tall and thin, with perfect cheekbones. I want perfect hair. I want all the girls in my class to wish they were me."

"Pah! Perfect, perfect, perfect. What is perfect?" Madame made an impatient gesture. "Perfection is not human, my dear. It is cold, it does not feel, it does not love. Look at me. Am I perfect? No, but I am magnificent!" The old witch stood and threw out her arms. In that instant, she was truly magnificent.

Martha was unmoved. She had heard stories about Madame Babatskaya, stories she had dismissed as urban legend, but now hoped with all her heart were true. She stood, too, and faced the dressmaker.

"Please. I want to be perfect, to be admired. It's all that I want. I can pay you."

Madame smiled. She knew this silly girl would not listen to the voice of experience. Some people are like that, never at home in their own skins, never happy with the splendid gifts given them. She agreed to give Martha what she wanted more than anything.

As prom approached, girls flooded the malls and the dress shops in giggly semi-hysterical search for their dream gowns. Every dressmaker in town was busy, but Madame Babatskaya's shop was the busiest of all. Word had gone round, and every teenaged girl and her mother had come to look at the dazzling gown in Madame's window display - the one on the gorgeous, willowy mannequin with the mane of shimmering hair. Everyone agreed the display was perfect.

Give Me Your Life

The snow tasted of nightmare. Roger tilted his face to the distant clouds and savored the cold bite of it, each spinning crystal sharp as a razor. He wished the delicate flakes were capable of slicing the life from him, of freeing him, but they only teased him with their feeble stings. He pulled up the collar of his coat and stepped from the alley.

A girl made her way along the snow-dusted pavement, keeping close to the curb and slipping a little in her stiletto heels. She gave her short skirt an angry tug and exhaled a plume of smoke with a soft curse. She reached the lamppost at the corner, made an almost military turn on her spiky heel, and reversed her parade along the street. When she saw Roger, she skidded to a stop, and the cigarette fell from its perch on her scarlet lip.

Roger watched the bright ember tumble the length of the girl's dark figure to lie winking at her feet. A moment stretched and yawned like a railway tunnel between them, and he could have had her. He could have stepped forward and slammed the heel of his hand under her chin. Could have bundled her into the dark alley and trussed her up like a Christmas fir. He had intended to do it. But the moment snapped, and the girl stepped sideways into the road and clicked away on her ridiculous heels as though she had just remembered an urgent appointment.

Roger leaned back into the shadows, put a trembling hand against the frigid bricks of the darkened building, and heaved a dry sob. It was always like this, night after night. He went out into the dark with his brain full of murderous thoughts, and his heart sick with dread that he would act on them. For the last three nights, he had stalked the prostitutes that worked along the river. He hated them, not for their mean lives, but for their unerring animal sense of survival. They never approached him, but strutted in a wide radius around him, their eyes sliding over him like the unseeing eyes of sleepwalkers. They avoided him like a bad smell. He would have to take rats back to the apartment again, or if he was lucky some skinny stray dog. He would have to face Daciana's relentless will, the agony as she peeled away more of his humanity, bent him inexorably to the yoke. Exhausted, he slumped against the wall.

It was odd to think that he had begun by *collecting* her. What a find he had thought her! The e-mail from Budapest had been sensational, Serge's excited message losing itself in typos. The antiquities dealer had found an ancient desiccated body in a tomb in the Romanian wilderness. It was, the burning message read, the mummified remains of a vampire. Roger had been on a plane within twenty-four hours. A day later, jet-lagged and haggard, he stood over the bundle of bones and rags and felt lust surge in his veins. The thing was beyond belief — a shrunken woman, bound in a tight ball with her knees drawn to her chest. The rope used to tie her was wound in thick loops around her wrists and ankles. Her head was bent sideways and leashed down onto her knees with a noose that would have made a hangman proud. Her skin was hard and leathery, weathered to a dull ivory, and her features were so shriveled and distorted as to be nearly unrecognizable as human. The eyes were closed, but one lid had curled up enough to allow the barest glimpse of a dark chitinous glitter. No orbs rolled in the long-dried sockets, but that hint of vital black had been unnerving. Serge had laughed when Roger drew back from the remains with a cry.

"Don't worry, my friend, she is very dead." Serge rapped the mummy along its curved spine with his knuckles, producing a wooden sound. "Pretty, eh? Look here, she has had her mouth stuffed with garlic. Bunch of superstitious bullshit!"

Roger stared at the thing's face, the long jaw agape and the bundle of rotten cloth jammed almost down the throat. Splinters of petrified garlic still jutted from the flimsy material ground between the full set of strong teeth. He bent closer.

"I don't see any fangs."

Serge guffawed. "You are an ass, Rog. Do you really believe the lady was a vampire? She was just some nobleman's wife who killed herself. Ate poison, so the story goes. Suicide was a great evil. The peasants weren't taking any chances."

"How do you know she was noble?"

Serge looked coy. "Well, her tomb, you know. And she was buried with some stuff that I was able to trace to a great house."

Roger straightened from his fascinated crouch, his collector's senses pinging. "What stuff?"

"Nothing much."

Roger gave Serge a steady, stern glare.

"Ok, ok. There were some jewels. I've got a buyer, so don't ask for them. I kept the mummy for you, and you'll never find another. Come on, Rog, a goddamned vampire! Talk about a folk culture artifact."

Serge rummaged through the spill of papers on his desk, and handed a sheaf of grainy photocopies to Roger. "Look. This authenticates her as Daciana, wife of Grigore the Wolf, a thirteenth century warrior and estate holder – sort of like a baron. That's solid research. Obviously, I can't give you a dealer's certificate on her. She's illegal as hell. I don't even know how you'll get her out of the country."

Roger grinned. "Let me worry about that."

The snow mesmerized him. In it were the memories of the vampire, memories of vast cold wilderness and violent rivers. With Daciana whispering in his head, he traveled backward through centuries to the dark medieval forests of her lifetime. Wolves ran through the falling snow, ghosting along under the flickering moon, intent on the hot red scent of prey fleeing panicked before them. He ran with them, a machine of bone and sinew, warm in his grizzled fur. Beneath his paws, he ground the snow and pine needle carpet to slurry. He did not know if the wind streamed howling past him, or if he flew like an arrow along its wintry track, lifted and hurled toward the panting deer with wild joy. The spurt of blood was orgasmic, and he came back to himself in a puddle made first red, then black, by the blinking neon above him. At his feet lay a woman, still quivering, and his hands were the slick gloves of a killer. It had happened finally, and he had not even been present.

The woman gave a last shuddering sigh. She was middle-aged, and wore glasses and a stocking cap with an enormous blue pom-pom. Her canvas bag spilled books onto the bricks. He looked around at the alley, noting details in the rhythmic strobe of the café sign. He was less than a block from his warehouse. If he dragged his victim to the gate at the rear of the alley, he could carry her along the darkened backs of the buildings and take her up to his apartment in the old delivery lift.

He looked down at her. She was small. He bent and got his hands under her shoulders, pulling her into a seated position against his legs. Her limbs sprawled and flopped, and her head rolled back causing the wound in her throat to laugh up at him. His hands felt stiff and sticky, and the woman felt colder than anything he'd ever touched. He dropped her and turned away, retching. He scrubbed at his hands with the end of his shirt, moaning softly, but voices from the street quieted him. People were leaving the café. The winking sign gave an angry sizzle and went dark or he might have been spotted, standing in the wet alley gutter with blood smeared from chin to crotch. Quick with adrenaline, he kicked the book bag into the deeper shadows and grabbed the dead woman by her collar, hauling her up against him and behind a dumpster. There he waited for the footfalls of the café patrons to recede, clasping his gory partner to his breast. Her lips touched his throat and he nearly screamed. Her flabby cold weight wanted to drag him down. Her breathless mouth gaped in dumb reproach. He knew he would never be able to carry her to the warehouse, desired nothing more than to hurl her from him, and he let her tumble down like an untethered marionette. He sank against the wall and crawled a few feet from her through the grimy snow, where he rolled himself into his overcoat and lay stunned.

He had been delighted, high on the excitement of his priceless acquisition, when he brought the vampire home. At once, he set to work in his shop and built a display case for her, balancing her frail rounded form on a cushion of sumptuous sable. He stared at her for days. Though he knew he must take pains to preserve her unmolested, he ached to touch her. He knew from his initial exploration of her skin that she was hard as teak, and smooth as a carved idol. Her teeth were robust. The living lady must have had a Hollywood smile and a good diet. Thinking of her enjoying a meal gave him a delicious shiver. He thought of her as "the vampire", and indulged in a freak-show mentality of equal parts fascination and disgust.

After a few days, he began to feel uncomfortable. The display case sat on a round Regency table in his library where he often slept by the fire, his books open all around him. He found that he had trouble concentrating on the lines of text before him. The fine hairs on the back of his neck would rise to attention, and although determined not to look at her, he would find himself glancing at the vampire with quick, covert looks from under his lashes. He could no longer sit in the chair by the fire, for her grotesque face was turned toward him there, and seemed to have assumed an avid watchfulness. The partially open eye glared like an inscrutable dark star, and so unsettled him that he draped the display case at night.

He began to have nightmares, waking in a sweat and gagging on the wild, coppery taste in his mouth. He stopped sleeping in the library, but it did no good. And still, his fingers itched to stroke the ancient flesh of the vampire. Finally, he removed her from the case and carried her to his workbench where he trained the magnifying light on her. She crouched in the harsh nimbus like a gargoyle, her feet gone to talons and her head turned at an impossible angle. She had been buried in a shroud, and it hung in stiff, fragile tatters around her skeletal ankles. It was drawn tight enough around her hips to show the shape of her pelvis, which was tiny. She must have been a diminutive woman. He swung the lens over her mouth, the jaw dislocated and pushed open and sideways by the brutality of the rope and of the fist-sized linen bundle of garlic. Despite his unease, he felt a stirring of pity for her. Before he thought about what he was doing, he reached out and tugged at the bundle. The rotted linen tore and puffed to dust in his fingers. The hard little knots of garlic spilled out and scattered over the workbench with a sound like the first fall of earth on a coffin lid. Startled, he leaped back. Into his mind, with the cruel precision of a surgeon's scalpel, came the voice. It was soft and implacable, and it spoke in a language unknown to him, yet he understood it perfectly.

It said, "Hunt."

The legends were true enough. It was blood she wanted, and he got it by killing his neighbors' dogs and cats until so many had disappeared that the police began to patrol the area heavily. He filled the guest bath and submerged her in the gore, and she softened and unfolded like a blossom opening its petals. For several weeks, she lay in the bath and sent him out to kill. She was weak, or he would have made a charnel house of the whole block. He was caught as an insect in amber, but he held on to the slippery rope of his own will and refused to bring her the human prey she demanded.

Returning with a briefcase stuffed with dead rats, he found her sitting up in the bath, her thin fingers clutching the porcelain rim. Her skin was white marble, clothed in diaphanous red. Blood clotted in the thick tangles of her hair. Her black eyes went to the briefcase, then to his face. For the first time, she spoke aloud.

"You mean to starve me. I will not allow it."

Shaken beyond words at her sudden show of vitality, he had tossed the rats by their tails into the horrible bath. The vampire pounced like a cat into the congealing blood and fished out her supper. She sank her teeth into the vermin and watched him over the carcasses as she fed. Roger took a slow, sliding step backward toward the door, and the vampire rose first to her knees and then to her feet, still sucking at the rats. Seconds later, she collapsed in a great splash of sticky crimson, and Roger fled. That had been two days ago. He had not been home, had not slept or eaten, had barely ceased his restless prowl of the city since then.

In the alley, Roger lay huddled against the café wall and watched the dead woman twitch on the snow. Rats. Already, they were finding their way into her coat, trying a nip here or there. He had come to know their habits well. He could rise and go over to the corpse and bludgeon a couple of the creatures for the vampire's meal, but he found he lacked any interest in the hunt now. He felt cold and hungry for the first time in weeks. The night seemed immense, crouching over him. He was friendless and worthless. He was a murderer. If he stayed in the alley, he would be found and imprisoned. He thought it would be best to go home, and he lurched up and staggered stiff-legged to the gate. He crept along the back walls of the buildings, and his shadow sloped along beside him, a towering hunched thing with its claws extended to the night. *It should be red*, he thought. Red was the color of his world.

He rode the lift to his apartment, clanking up out of the dark hell of the warehouse where his shadow had been swallowed by the heavier blackness. He missed it; it had seemed more alive than he, more purposeful. In the apartment, a single lamp cast its dim glow across the pale marble floors where small red footprints marched toward the library. Red. That was right; that was the order in his chaos. Roger followed the prints until they vanished in the scarlet pattern of the Persian carpet. Daciana stood looking at the display case on the round Regency table. She was naked, lean and ropy with sinew. Her rusty patina of blood was all the covering she needed, for she was a pure thing, an angel of primal terror. She turned when he entered and her face, as always, was expressionless.

"Come. Kneel. Give me your life," she said.

And he did.

Sweet May

When it became known that the Queen of Air and Storm would bring her court to the Wild Knob Woods for the annual Festival of Leaves, the exciting news whizzed across the long forested miles on birdsong. The trees clacked and whispered, knocking their grey antlers together in their rush to festoon themselves with the finest sashes of scarlet creeper. Those who had not yet begun to blush with autumnal fire meditated on russet, gold, and crimson until the green faded from their raiment and they blazed like torches against the peerless blue sky. All of them strove for dignified perfection of form and hue, rustling and creaking with the effort. They were old, proud trees that had seen many things, but none of them had ever seen the Queen.

None was prouder than Sweet May, tall and strong, with sugar in her veins and a canopy of sublime aspect. Her swaying foliage of clear gold and pale orange was a handsome counterpoint to her shapely silver trunk. Her limbs were like the arms of a goddess. She was the darling of Wild Knob Woods. As the forest feverishly prepared for the arrival of the royal court, Sweet May stood calmly in the dappled sun and dreamed of how the Queen would favor her above all the other trees (for if Sweet May had a fault, it was vanity).

At last, the wonderful day arrived. First came the Queen's heralds, the Order of Zephyrs, mounted on lean white horses. They frisked through the Woods, piping and laughing, happy as children. The golden balm of the sun came with them, and the trees basked in it, enjoying the first scattering of leaves like gentle puffs of confetti. Sweet May turned her gaze inward and tossed down only a few paltry leaves. She didn't want to waste her beauty on these clowning servants.

Next came the noble court in chariots of brisk wind. The sky billowed like a blue sail and the clouds raced by, dragging their fleecy bellies across the reaching fingers of the trees. With the court came the sound of horns and whistles, and the courtiers galloped past the delighted trees with such force that the leaves whirled away in waltzing spirals before fluttering in bright curtains to the ground. Even Sweet May hummed with pleasure at the pomp and pageantry, allowing a gust of shimmering gold to fly from her branches. She could see the Queen's open carriage topping the hill, and was giddy with anticipation.

But, oh, how shocked Sweet May was at her first sight of the Queen! The monarch was ancient beyond even the ken of the trees, her long white hair tangled and wild, her eyes empty and hard as ice. Her robes were tattered and streamed behind her in a great gale. The carriage she rode in was plain hammered metal; her horses were snorting brutes of night. Sweet May shivered in the sudden cold of disappointment. Was this ragged harridan the Queen?

The brisk glittering court and the frolicking Zephyrs grew still and fell to their knees. A blustery fellow in a cloak of cirrus began to call out, "Bow down! Bow down, all you subjects! Bow down before the Queen of Air and Storm!"

His voice was that of rising weather, and his thin cloak smoked and grew dark. The trees of Wild Knob Woods were nothing if not weather-wise, and awestruck in the presence of the great Queen, they bent their hoary backs. All but Sweet May, who stood tall and proud as ever.

"I will not bow to that ugly old crone," said she. "Why, I am far more beautiful than this so-called Queen. Perhaps it is she who should bow down."

A murmur of horror swept through the court at this defiance. The Queen pulled up her foaming horses and turned her empty, icy eyes upon Sweet May. Her mouth stretched open in a terrible wail, her hair rose like lightning into the angry sky, and her torn and colorless robes writhed about her in a roiling fog. A howling wind rushed upon the Woods and slammed into the ranks of trees, rolling over their bent backs and tearing the remaining leaves from their branches. Twigs, nuts, even small stones flew about. The forest floor was cleared as if by a giant broom. In the midst of this pandemonium, there was a loud *crack!* that struck fear into the hearts of the cowering trees.

Bit by bit, the storm subsided. When the trees dared to straighten themselves to their full height again, they found they had been stripped naked and that the Queen and her court were gone. The festive Woods was bare of color; the sky was leaden and smelled of snow. Winter had come scratching at the seasonal door. The birds were silent. And Sweet May was broken at her proud waist, condemned to bow down forever after.

The Exchange

The heart that sustains me is not my own, but that of my younger sister. I never meant to steal it, no matter what anyone says. It came to me as a gift, and mine went out with the limbs and lumps. To feel the strength of it, even through the pain of surgery, even though I am scarred as an autopsy subject, is a marvel. More than that, it is a triumph.

Angela and I were eighteen months apart. My parents worked quickly to shore up their hopes with a healthy girl against the treachery of my defect. My heart was weak, a fluttering, flabby sac that did its work listlessly. As soon as I was able to understand, I began the wait for the inevitable - for the day that my heart would cease even the pretense of interest in the tidal flow of my blood. That is a heavy burden for a child, to feel death stalking about the rooms after me like a cat with a mouse.

For me survival was a matter of languidness, both physical and emotional. I was stoical and dull. I rarely laughed and never argued. I moved like an elder, careful and slow, pausing often to appraise the internal weather of my heart. Angela was my reverse. She had an immense capacity for life, and the accompanying appetite for it, voracious and unheeding. She never thought about her quick grace or her easy laughter. She was simply open to the world, in love with the vitality she was a part of, and loved in return. As we forged into our teens, she radiated beauty and promise.

I was Angela's ghost, the recipient of her cast off clothing, the slow tag-along, plump and breathless. We shared a room, and Angela was my watcher. As my heart could stutter to a halt anytime, she was urged to vigilance, but it was I who heeded heartbeats in the shadowed hours. Night after night, I lay and listened to the steady drum of her heart in the wooly dark. I imagined I could feel the hot current of her blood rushing through my veins, the power of strong limbs stroking back the quilt, my body a rising nation and every cell a vital citizen. I imagined myself inside her skin, flushed and glowing, burning with life. I imagined resting in the knowledge that each morning was a blossom opening to me, offering its beauty and fragrance, the sweet drop of time, time, time. Most of all, I imagined that constant engine that flared and ebbed within her ribs, the red promise of it. My own heart shuddered and jerked, and pushed life sluggishly through my cold body. I felt heavy and weak, my limbs inert slabs of meat, faintly lavender under their wax white surfaces. If Angela was a tawny cat, curling and stretching in the heat of her own pelt, I was a corpse. Sleep was a terror best avoided, and so for fifteen years I listened each night to the poisonous din of my sister's heart.

There were compensations. I found infinite worlds in books and read everything I got my hands on. My parents fed them to me, shoveling knowledge into my brain as though stoking a furnace, and I consumed them. By my sixteenth birthday, I had graduated from high school and embarked on my college career. My computer was my campus, and though it was a disappointment not to be allowed the thrill of actual classrooms and the stimulation of fellow students, I had become accustomed to living a virtual life. While Angela played soccer and led the cheerleading squad, I traveled the world. In our darkened bedroom, the computer screen was a glowing doorway through which I eagerly slipped. That was how I found The Shrouded Market.

It was both a philosophy and a marketplace for the most obscure esoterica on the planet. It was where I was introduced to the oldest gods, some whose names had been lost many thousands of years ago and whose purposes are only conjecture. Death is only a portal for them; they travel from the lands beyond it that are unfathomable to us. The Shrouded Market taught me how to call upon these gods and how to pay for what I wanted. I wanted life, Angela's life, and so the exchange was a simple one, really.

Our parents bought a summer house on Icehouse Lake in Blackfern County. It is the only house on the lake besides the Blackfern Lodge which is hidden from view by a great jutting cliff thickly wooded in pines. The real estate agent had to disclose to us that three people had died there in a period of less than three years. She couldn't very well have kept it a secret. The village of Wickeford Mills lies twelve miles away, and is a hive of local gossip. My mother was dismayed that Angela and I had heard the story, but I realized at once that it was the first sign that one of the ancient gods had heard my petition. The house was a special place — the perfect place, in fact, for the exchange. While my parents stood on the deck and exclaimed over the view of the lake and the floating dock, I asked the house agent where the bodies had been found.

She was uncomfortable, yet I could see the blood avidity in her eyes that told me she wanted to talk about the deaths.

"The first was a man; he had a heart attack and drowned in the lake. Then a young woman bought the place. She died in her sleep, another heart attack they think, in the bedroom at the end of the hall. Another woman was found dead in the library, also apparently of a heart attack." The agent smacked her lips. "Weird, huh? All those heart attacks?"

I nodded, but I didn't think it was weird at all. It was a god talking, confirming the power of this place and the acceptance of my proposed payment. We followed my parents and Angela down to the lake.

On the end of the dock that bobbed gently in the lake's smooth surf was an anchor stone, a rough round of concrete with the rusted loop of an eye bolt jutting crookedly from its top. The chain that had once secured it to the cleats of a rowboat hung from it over the end of the dock and down into the clear blue water, like a corroded bell pull. I wondered what it might summon if tugged. I put my foot on the anchor stone and felt how it rocked as the lake water slapped at the dock. It was very close to the edge, but heavy and irregular enough not to roll off. The heavy submerged links of chain seemed to chime, signaling the rightness of the place, and I turned my face into the wind and let it lift my lank hair.

"Olivia! Come away from the water! Do you want to fall in?"

My mother snapped her fingers at me as though she were chastising a dog. I trudged back to shore, noting as I went that Angela was climbing over the tumbled stones at the water's edge and getting her sneakers wet as she looked for fossils. Her long legs were already starting to tan in the late spring sun. No one called her back.

Summer at the lake was magical. I soaked it in, enjoying it more than any other summer of my life up till then because I knew that all I observed would soon be mine. The Shrouded Market told me to immerse myself in thoughts of the thing I desired, so I reveled in the clean spicy smell of the lake, the heat of the sun, and the sighing of the wind in the tall pines. I spent more time outdoors than I ever had before, and I watched Angela. Yes, most of all I observed my sister, who was sun-browned and strong. I watched her run on her long brown legs. I watched her paint her toenails bubblegum pink. I watched her slide across the face of the lake in the kayak Dad bought for her, and I noted the lean muscles of her arms. Her face was flushed with summer, and I thought she had never been more beautiful or more vibrant. I especially liked to watch her swim, and soon it became our routine to go down to the dock together, she in her swimsuit and I with my book. As she swam, I sat on the warm planks with my feet dangling in the water and held the book in my lap, but I wasn't reading. I was memorizing Angela. Every so often, I would rest my bare foot on the rough surface of the anchor stone and rock it gently.

One night, I looked from our bedroom window and saw the moon squatting by the side of the lake. It was an enormous bloody sphere, so near it frightened me until I realized it was a reflection. Looking up, I saw the actual satellite glowering down from low on the ridge. The moon and its reflection made a pair of burning red eyes in a titanic dark face, and they stared at me with hungry expectancy. The breath shriveled in my lungs, and as I stood paralyzed at the window, some unseen creature shattered the calm of the lake with its splashing. The visitation was ended, but I knew it was time to make the exchange.

The next day was blue and gold with the spirit of summer. I was calm. I had no difficulty waiting until the afternoon to go with Angela down to the lake. Just as The Shrouded Market had foretold, events moved inevitably to their conclusions. The exchange could not have been halted even if I had wished it. Angela dashed out onto the dock and dove into the water, her body like a knife. I took my place at the end of the planks beside the anchor stone. As the slight wash from her dive reached the dock, the rusty chain that hung in the water rang like a subtle bell. She did her laps, then swam over to me and turned on her back. The dock rode high on the water, maybe as much as two feet above its surface, and I looked down at her and pulled my feet up.

"Angela, do you know if Dad called the satellite technician? My internet's down again."

"Mmm hmm."

Her eyes were closed and she floated a little closer, the shadow of the dock darkening her face like a blindfold.

"He should be here soon. Dad's going to -"

The splash of the anchor stone was tremendous. There was a crunching thud and then the burbling whoosh of the water filling the sudden vacuum made by Angela's body as it was forced under by that concrete weight. Her limbs flailed out once, as though she were about to dive, and then she didn't move. The lake turned vermilion in an instant.

I hung over the dock, stretched on my belly, and reached for her arm - white now instead of bronze, because all the color had been let out of her. The lake is very cold, even in high summer. It had once been a mine, but when the miners hit the subterranean river that flooded it, it was as if they had unleashed a living creature. Its sinuous, heavy body had filled the pit in minutes, drowning all of them.

I gasped as the chill took my hand, and I pawed at Angela's slick shoulder, trying to fish her upward, trying to see if her eyes were open now. My fingers paddled through the floating strands of her hair. Her head rolled on a boneless neck, her face turning toward the brilliant sky. It was slack as a dreamer's, the eyes half closed and flatly shimmering as beads of mercury. A bit of her skull flexed outward as I tugged my fingers out of the web of her crimson hair. Purple black bruises were filling the hollows of her eyes. Suddenly she gave a hoarse snorting breath and water gushed from her mouth.

The lake and the sky revolved. I felt that I was floating over the water like a soap bubble. Voices came close and receded, then blared in distress. Dad had found us. He wasn't alone; a burly man in khaki shorts and a white shirt thrust his way past me. His name tag shouted TED in thick black embroidery. Angela rose from the lake, pointing accusingly toward me as her crooked head lolled on the white shoulders, turning them red. Ted shouted instructions, and Dad sprinted for the house. Soon he and Mom were both back, hefting a cooler between them. The three of them packed Angela in ice like a picnic lunch and wrapped her head in white towels that turned scarlet with the speed of a magic trick.

More men arrived, big men in baseball caps and tee shirts with the sleeves torn off. With infinite care, they moved Angela and her bags of ice to a blanket. Between them they lifted her and carried her to a van that read "Dark's Nursery" on the side and drove her away. They drove me away, too, in a pickup bearing the same logo, struck as dumb and immobile as my stubbornly un-dead sister.

At Our Lady of the Mount Hospital in St. John's Port, Angela was pronounced brain dead. Hooked to the arcane machinery in the house of medicine, her body still breathed and her heart still pumped, but it was a ruse. Angela was dead, and my payment had been remitted. I lay on a gurney in the ER, listening to my heart monitor beep querulously, and waiting for the exchange. I didn't know what form it would take. I mean that. I didn't know they would harvest her heart, or that I would be lying naked and unaware in a surgical theater within the hour. Whatever else I am now, I'm not a thief.

The Bear

The hunters gathered around the big fire in the cold dawn. Sleepy village wives watched blearily from the doorways, bouncing babies on their angular hips. The men were dressed in heavy fur parkas and stout boots, the ancient bear spears clutched in their hands. The spears were taller than the men, with heavy brutal heads of steel. The men didn't talk, each one swallowing his fear with the cold air.

The men were young, dark-bearded. Their faces were already hardened and lined like the faces of their fathers who circulated among them, doling out solemn bits of advice, checking and re-checking the weapons, urging courage in the face of this impossible task. One of these young men would be chosen and marked by the bear, would return with the beast god's fire burning through his veins to take up his mantle as village healer. The others...

A sixth figure, bundled in furs like the rest but without a weapon, walked toward the group through the thin mist and the smoke of the cook fires. The men eyed it and turned away. This hunter did not belong, either to the village or to the tradition. A woman from outside, she had a long red braid that hung out of her hood like a sleeping snake and a freckled skin like milk dusted with nutmeg. She waited silently outside the knot of men, unperturbed by their snubbing. The watching wives did not speak, yet a kind of murmur passed among them like a breeze. It was not unheard of for women to attend the hunt for the great bear, but it had been many generations since one had been marked a healer, and never had an outsider made the attempt.

A grandfather approached the woman, his stern face toughened by the years into an impassive leather mask. He stood looking at her, and she returned his gaze. The other men turned to watch the exchange.

"You will be killed. Why go?" His voice was soft as a sigh. He shook his head and spat on the ground. "You have no weapons."

The woman, who had clenched her fear into an icy ball in her middle, looked toward the dark spruce mountains. The mist rose in silver scarves from them, and they seemed to breathe winter onto the air.

"I will go because I must. I don't need a weapon. Do you understand about my dream?"

The old man nodded. He had heard the dream, the night message that had brought the woman here from her faraway life. He did not discount such things. He reached out and clasped her slight shoulder.

"I do not think I will see you again, but listen now. Face the bear with bravery. When it is your turn, do not run." He gave a curt nod and walked back to his house, to his breakfast and his morning routine. If the outland woman sacrificed herself to the bear, it was not because she hadn't been warned.

The hunters climbed the narrow path in single file, the harsh sawing of their breath written on the air. The woman followed, last in line, ignored but not forgotten. The men held to a steady pace she could keep up with, their one unspoken courtesy. It was cold, and the ground was stony. They were above the slender tops of the spruces. Snow lay in thin crystalline patches, curled into the small root hollows, and fell in spiraling flakes that clung to her eyelashes. She could smell the frozen earth, the sharp and dusty fragrance of cold stone, and the sweet conifers. Looking up, she could see the top of the ridge, razor sharp against a grieving sky. She could see the entrance to the cave.

As the first hunter set his boot on the bare earth in front of the cave, a roar shook the trees. They all froze, their blood froze, their hearts froze, six small people turned to stone at the tremendous voice of the Forest King. The men made sure of their grasps on their spears. They would enter the cave one by one, like supplicants, but ready to do battle. *Don't go in*, the woman thought. *Oh, god, don't go in there.* But they did go in. One after another, the hard young men went in, and none of them came out. Then it was her turn.

She stepped to the mouth of the cave. Inside, the floor was fine silted earth, clean and bare as a ballroom. Against the walls, rolled and tumbled like discarded playthings, were the five hunters. Carnage. Her eyes grew wide, and the icy pellet of fear in her stomach expanded and sent its tentacles out into her veins. She looked up from the floor of the cave and the creature that dwelled there stood, up and up, towering and roaring. It was no bear. It looked like a bear. It had a hot, red gullet and the claws and teeth of a bear. It was dark as death, and massive in the way of a bear, but she made no mistake. This was an elemental god, and she was stupid for coming here. She would never leave.

The bear god's voice shivered her skull and dissolved her will. In one rapid, elegant sweep of its shaggy arm, it gathered her to it and shook her. Something snapped, and she felt nothing. Pain was beyond her, and she surrendered, draped like a limp fairy tale princess over the deadly claws.

"See how easily it is done."

The voice was deep and easy, hard as granite and faintly amused. All her fear fled at the sound of it, and she was happy. Happy to be taken down to her fundamental parts by this great mechanic. Deft claws hooked her skin and unzipped it from her like a wetsuit, turned her inside out and counted her bones.

When the woman woke, she was alone. The cave was empty of all but the wind that sang in its throat. She rose, re-assembled in proper order, and began the long walk back to the village.

Bluebeard Revisited

﹡﹡﹡

Weddings and funerals, mused Madame Babatskaya, are occasions for the most elaborate attention to detail. Take, for instance, the funeral she was to attend that very day. A lavish affair with a carriage hearse and four black horses to draw it, dark plumes on their heads like pinions from the wings of Death himself. A somber sequel to an opulent wedding not four days celebrated, the bride in a gown of Madame's design (a confection of tightly laced satin and crystal-encrusted embroidery as piercingly crisp as the first snowflake of Russian winter), the corpulent groom dark and splendid as a crow. Now the bride, a great-niece of Madame's, lay in her velvet-lined casket in the drafty church awaiting her admirers once again. A narrow bed indeed for one who, in life, had such a fear of confined spaces that her own corset was an object of terror.

Sighing, Madame sat before the gigantic moon of her dressing table mirror and began laboriously to wind and pin her jet hair into an extravagant tower of dizzying whorls. She thought about the wedding in a languid way as she spun and piled and pinned her hair. And as she thought, the clock upon the mantel slowed and the candles ceased their steady melt. Madame brought her great intuition and formidable knowledge of human weakness to bear upon a troubling point of memory, something small. A slub in the weave of the tapestry, difficult to find in the larger pattern, but liable to unravel the whole.

Madame remembered that she hadn't cared for the groom's looks, though he was as richly caparisoned as the king's own mount, his horrid beard combed and strewn with seed pearls. Madame knew a goat when she saw one, and the Count had the glazed yet simmering aspect of a randy ram, his libertine's eyes already tearing the bodice of his bride's exquisite gown. No silk cravat impaled with pigeon's egg ruby, no figured waistcoat in shades of storm and nightmare, no luscious froth of ashen lace pouring like a midnight tide from raven cuffs could disguise his awful nature. He was incandescent with lust and cruelty. Madame, applying rouge and lip paint in her frozen mirror, made a moue of distaste. It was an unpleasant memory, but, no...that wasn't the flaw she sought.

Shaking out the floating shadows of her peignoir, Madame rang for her morning chocolate. She remembered that the Count had been married before, and widowed, no less than six times. Scandalous! His wives seemed a peculiarly accident prone lot, falling under carriages or from trains in blizzards, drowning in vats of champagne, throwing themselves from their opera boxes. One had set herself alight in the boxwood labyrinth (strolling in the twilight between the luminaries, her trailing robes and scarves had snatched fire as handily as Prometheus). Tsk, tsk. Madame drew her own diaphanous sleeve away from the candelabrum. These...accidents, they were closer to what tickled her witch's nose.

The maid brought the sweet and steaming cup, her dour face like punched bread dough enough to curdle the cream. Madame addressed the maid's reflection as the chocolate was set upon the dressing table.

"Agnes, do you recall the wedding of the Count and the unfortunate chit I go to see buried today?"

Agnes did indeed recall it, for hadn't she helped to dress the girl, all thin flanked and shivering on the morn of her marriage to the great house. Not given to oratory, the maid nodded.

"Did you not say you had seen the Count in the village earlier that day?"

Again, Agnes made an affirmative bob of her head. After a long, slender minute she thought to add, "I seen him coming from the chemist's shop, and right skulking he looked, too. Not a bit like a man on his wedding day." In a paroxysm of loquacity, Agnes charged on. "To think that poor girl done poisoned herself. It's tragic, is what."

Ah! In a sudden whirlwind of decisive action, Madame leaped to her groaning wardrobe and brought out her funeral finery. The mantel clock began to tick loudly and the candles slouched in rapid demise. Agnes hove to and corseted the old lady. In a blink, Madame was dressed, wasp-waisted and uncompromisingly erect, her Himalaya of ebon hair attenuating her spidery physique until she resembled, in her unrelieved black, a shadow that stretches up the wall. Her only jewelry was a wide bracelet of old gold adorned by a soft oval of dark taffeta fattened with wool, an aristocratic tailor's friend, a cushion in which was sunk a single pearl-eyed pin of wicked fineness. This she hid beneath her long lace cuff.

"Ring for the horses, Agnes. I go to a funeral." Madame chuckled. "Yes, such a funeral we shall have."

The church was cold and damp. Madame, fortified against the chill with immense furs and a silver flask of brandy, glided to the front pew and descended to a seated position. At the opposite end of the pew sat the Count, his fleshy face a lugubrious waxwork, his beard crackling upon his shirt front with evil energy. The man's eyes devoured the pallid form of his dead bride in much the same way as on their wedding day, a gaze both rapacious and bored. Madame thought of her kitchen cat, and the way it watched the futile creeping of the mice along the baseboard, weighing the advantages of the chase against the expenditure of force. Rising, she went to the casket and looked upon the face of her great-niece, a silly girl with an abundance of romantic fluff between her ears. Still, Madame felt a family obligation.

With the suavity of a stage magician, Madame withdrew the shining pin from the tailor's cushion beneath her cuff and pricked the dead girl's white hand. A miniscule bead of blood bedewed the hand, and so Madame determined that her relative was not dead at all, an intuitive conclusion she had arrived at in her boudoir and that had wanted only this simple proof. No, the girl was not dead, not yet. Her fate was to be interred alive in the crypt beneath the church, the cruelest horror for such a claustrophobe. And there, seated on the aisle and wearing his theatrical mask of sorrow, was the architect of that horror, the connoisseur of cruelties, the gourmand of piquant murder. His very beard bristled with diabolical delight.

Madame patted the cool hand of the girl in the casket, then turned and made her slow, mournful way up the aisle. As she passed the Count, she drew a handkerchief from her cuff to dab her eyes, and in her grief and great age, she stumbled. The Count reached out to steady her, murmuring insincere words of condolence, he knew she had been close to her niece, had taught her to sew. Madame clung for a moment, light as a cobweb, to the thick slab of his arm.

Her dry bony fingers brushed against his wrist as she found her strength and moved on toward the tall doors of the church. The little tailor's cushion, hidden in the tumble of her lace, was empty. The pin, fine as a hair and sharp as true love's dart, was sliding unfelt through the blue vein of the Count's wrist. It raced through his body on the swift tide of his blood until it came to the engine of his heart where it lodged with the finality of a bullet. During its journey, Madame walked toward the daylight, each step firmer and more graceful than the last, the erect figure gaining stature and vigor, until the Count fell dead and Madame shrugged her furs from her shoulders and strode into pale sunlight.

Four sturdy footmen awaited her. As she stepped into her carriage, she paused and looked them over, then glanced back at the church that was buzzing like a hive stirred with a stick.

"Gentlemen," Madame addressed the footmen, "bring out my niece. Leave the casket."

Death Is No Land For The Weak

❧

The first thing you need to know is that I knew I was dead. That's important, because I'm not claiming I was lost or confused. It's true that I had a sudden death, the kind the psychics like to say creates an angry spirit, or a stupefied one that wanders around moaning. I can remember the event, but it doesn't hold any charge for me. It's like it happened in a movie. I'd been working on my ninth book - which I guess is a wash now. My agent probably shit a brick. I don't really know, because I was gone for quite a while — just floating in limbo, I guess. I can't remember that part, but when I got back the dying part was crystal clear.

Anyway, I had been hammering out the chapters, each scene burning through me the way it does (*did*) when the lines to the great cosmic story vault are wide open and humming. I wanted to immerse myself in that flow, and I wanted to turn off everything else in my life for a while. Things were messy. My girlfriend had left me, and I'd responded to that stressor by showing up half drunk and all nasty for a live radio interview. I continued my reign of bad behavior deep into the night by drinking myself stupid and busting up a roadside bar. I got two nights in the county lockup for that lapse in decorum.

I'm not proud of it. I blame the August heat. It was relentless and heavy with humidity, summer going out with a snarl. I'd always hated that time of year, the stifling stickiness of it and the dull glare of the idiot sun. Candace leaving when she did was like a brief frost in hell. The air conditioning in my building was bogged down again, and all there was to relieve the awful heat was a sluggish current of clammy semi-cooled air that smelled faintly of mildew. The heat didn't bother Candace, who never seemed to sweat.

"I think it's time to call it quits, Eddie," she said. Coolly, like she was reading a grocery list. Pick up eggs and butter, dump Ed and piss on his character.

When I asked why, when I wondered what had happened, she gave me a pitying look that said, *oh, you simple creature.* Then she lit a cigarette and squinted at me through the ascending blue scarf of smoke.

"You really are a self-absorbed bastard. Look, I'm leaving now. I've got no more time for the Ed Spencer show. Don't call me. Just go fall into one of your horrible stories and have a ball."

That hurt. They say that death is the great equalizer. Well, we'll see.

With the book coming in loud and clear on all frequencies (*the Ed Spencer Show, ladies and gentlemen - all Eddie, all the time*), I'd decided to get out of town and sequester myself in the house on Pine Knob. There above the lake, I could look out the glass walls and watch the woods fill in everything all the way to the horizon.

It seemed like a good decision. Icehouse Lake cast its glacial aura far enough into the simmering pines to blunt the hot knife of the sun. I settled down and got my head together. The quiet, which is huge and somehow sentient, got in my veins like a calmative. I like to think I was a pretty tightly-wrapped dude – not high tension wrapping, but the well-adjusted lacing of a rational man. I like to think I was the kind of guy who people say is easy-going. I shouldn't be remembered for a little caveman blip on the radar. The time at Pine Knob seemed to glue me back together in short order, self-absorbed bastard that I was. I wrote, I swam in the lake that was like iced silk, I watched sunsets from the deck, my bare feet talking amicably with the smooth sun-warmed cedar planks and a cold bottle of beer chilling my fingers. I even had a civil phone conversation with Candace who, with a reptilian lack of passion, called to discuss the division of assets jointly accrued during our relationship. She phrased it just that way.

I was forty-six when I died, and in damn good shape for a man my age. I hit the gym, I ran, I swam. I think I can be pardoned for believing my heart was ox-strong. It had never given me reason to think otherwise. That fateful day in late August, when I dove off the dock into the frigid arms of the lake, I was looking forward to the sizzle of a steak on the grill and to popping the cork on a robust red when I finished my afternoon laps. I swam out, far enough to feel the dead cold of the depths gripping my legs all the way to the thighs as I stopped to tread water and to look back at the dock. I was still a long way from the middle. Icehouse is big, and it falls away fast to appalling depths. It started out as a mine, and the miners had made considerable headway in their delving to Hades when the water started gushing in, rolling in like a vast sinuous sea serpent, eating them up. So I'm not alone down there in the black.

When the heart attack hit me, I was bobbing half on the warmer surface where the sun had some power and half in the outer-space iciness that seemed to spear upward from the void. I felt my heart seize like a clenched fist and turn to stone. It was heavier than a stone, though, a concentrated density with the crushing power of a black hole. It sucked in the world, which dwindled rapidly to a small glaring white dot, and then winked out. I couldn't shout or even lift an arm, not that it would have done me any good. The only other place on the lake is Blackfern Lodge, too far away and hidden from view by jutting points of wilderness. I went down unremarked, *glug*, like the fucking Titanic - feet first for the bottom. It took a long time to reach it, and I drowned along the way, but it wasn't as bad as it sounds. I wasn't feeling much except surprise. And then, for a long time, I didn't feel or know anything.

The second thing you need to know is that desire is a stealth weapon. Out of a guileless blue sky it clobbers you, and your ass goes up in a mushroom cloud of greedy need. I'd felt it when I was the old flesh and bones me, sure, but after I died I thought I was done with all that. I am, after all, a shade of my former self. *Da dum dum.* I'm not saying that absolves me of my wrongs. But then, I no longer seek absolution, and that is a stone-cold relief.

When I first came back to the lake house, I felt like a man shaking off a hangover. Wobbly, a bit disconnected. I remembered the heart attack and the drowning the way I might have once recalled an embarrassing drunken flirtation. It seemed that I had opened my eyes after a brief nap and found myself standing on the dock dressed in jeans and a Hard Rock Café t-shirt. My wet swim trunks were gone, but I was still barefoot. August was gone as well. The trees were in full autumn regalia, and the smooth sapphire surface of the lake had become a rumpled grey sheet under speeding twists of cloud. Everything looked brisk and cold, but I couldn't feel it.

A squadron of Canada geese came honking in for a landing, and splashed around a bit before floating serenely up and down on the mild chop. I watched them for a minute, and then I tried to dive off the dock - a momentary lapse during which I thought if I could reunite with my body I might crawl back inside it and make it work again. I was unable to free myself from one element in favor of another, though. Earth had my spirit as surely as the Icehouse had my bones, and every time I jumped I landed on the rough planks of the dock. Lying on my stomach, I reached down to the fierce wavelets, and I couldn't even touch them. They glided away from my hand in a sly oily way that frightened me.

Above me, the house loomed against the moody sky like the dark prow of a ship. I turned my back on the unfriendly lake and made my way up to the deck, now bare of outdoor furniture, and went inside. I didn't think about it. It was my house, and I just reached out and opened the door. If I had known it would only work one way, that I would be unable to leave, I wonder if I would have gone in. I wonder how different my story would have been.

The house was empty of furniture and possessions. I was shocked all over again. Then I was angry. Candace and I had owned the lake house together, and although I had agreed to buy her out after our breakup, I hadn't had time to take care of it. Staring at the barren rooms, I could see that upon finding herself the sole owner, she had allowed no grass to grow under her feet. I went through the place like a wind, stirring up whispering echoes with my passage. Nothing. She'd left nothing! How could she even presume I was dead?

I rushed from room to room, cursing and shaking. I ended up in the kitchen, staring at the calendar on the wall, a freebie from the local bank that featured photos of the area. It was turned to October, showcasing a big golden starburst of a maple with a stranglehold on the boulders at its roots, but it was the year that caught my horrified eye. It told me, in assertive bold type, that I had been dead for more than two years. It told me that the last week of a long-ago August was the least of what had slipped my grasp. I glanced out the window at the brilliant leaves, many on the trees but many more in enormous crispy drifts on the ground. I thought it must be at least mid-month and felt the shivery finger of delirium tickle me.

It was one thing to be dead, but another to meditate on the idea of my body rising from the Icehouse depths like a terrible helium balloon, nibbled by fish, waxy and bloated and purple. Yes, it was another thing altogether to think of some pimply-faced sheriff's deputy fishing me out of the lake with a boathook, maybe yurking over the side of the little police outboard because of the smell. To think of the black envelope of a body bag waiting on the dock, like a flabby detached shadow. I could imagine it all with gruesome clarity.

A cramp seized me, and I bent double, stunned to feel anything. I didn't know what it was then, or what it would take to eradicate it. If I'd still had guts to twist and stab, that's what I would have said it felt like. As it abated, I staggered upright feeling thin and fragile. Hollow. I thought that if someone were to strike me, I would ring like a bell or shatter like a thin plaster veneer. I could feel the lack of life inside me — not the presence of death, but a vacuum where nothing existed. I had no comparable experience, and so at first I thought I was hungry. Turns out, I wasn't wrong.

Time is elastic when you're dead. On the one hand, it seems to fill the known universe with a great white nothingness, extending outward from a single point (me, in this case) in all directions and dimensions. There is so much of it that it begins to feel weighty, as though rather than streaming *from* that central point, it is funneling *into* it like the surge of a violent sea squeezing through a narrow estuary. The mass of it sometimes felt like it would blow me apart, as if I would simply burst and flow away on its infinite slow currents.

One the other hand, time is small and fast, like a cockroach. Occurrences come lurching up out of the fog, then glide away at speed before they can be grasped and interpreted. This was more distressing to me because I felt as though things were sneaking up on me, jumping out at me like pranksters from around dark corners.

I had wandered about the house for a while, feeling trapped and bored. It didn't seem like a long time to me, maybe an hour or two, but when I glanced outside I saw a snowy morning and naked trees. The lake was frozen, gone the milky blue color of a dead eye. Time had leaped forward without me. That shook me up, and I went to a corner of the empty library and slid onto the floor with my back against the bare shelves. I put my head down and sobbed.

I hadn't cried since I was a kid. I was overwhelmed with that cramping hollow feeling, and I was starting to feel cold, too. I could no longer suffer the misery of a chilled body. Instead, I felt like vapor ghosting off a block of dry ice. I was drifting apart - I was suddenly sure of it - and the desire to remain shot through me with such ferocity that I bolted to me feet.

That was when I saw the girl for the first time. From the corner of my eye I caught movement, a flashing glimpse of a young woman on a library stool stretching upwards to place books on a high shelf. I shouted in surprise and fell over my own feet, tumbling to the floor that, for just a moment, was covered with a thick Persian carpet. In an instant, it was all gone. I was alone with empty shelves, on my ass on the bare plank floor. I sat there and thought about what had just happened, and an idea began to form.

The next time I saw her, I was in the kitchen. I was sitting on the built-in banquette, staring morosely out the window at the snow, when I heard a light-hearted laugh. I turned toward the sound and saw the girl for a fleeting instant, leaning against the counter with the phone nestled between her ear and her shoulder. She was peeling an orange. I leaped up, but the vision was gone, as though it had slid behind a wall like a stage set on wheels.

After that, I had another experience in the library when I walked into an invisible object that materialized, bit by bit, into a piano. It sat where my desk had once been. I reached out and touched a key, and the baby grand spoke. It stayed where it was, too, and I plinked up and down the keyboard before it vanished, melting away like fog instead of winking out of existence like a magic trick. As it was dissolving, a frightened voice whispered beside my ear, *Oh god, it's happening again.*

The final thing you need to know is that accidental evil is still evil, all the way to its core. I know that now. I'm figuring out a few things about this after-life, but I sure don't have all the answers. One thing I've learned is that you have to act ruthlessly or vanish forever - compassion is a useless currency. Death is no land for the weak.

After the incident with the piano, everything fell into place for me. Illumination in the darkness, and that's pretty funny when you consider my first meal as a dead man. I got the idea that the house was like a palimpsest of memories - my memories - imperfectly erased and overwritten by current happenings. I was now sure that a new resident existed in the same rooms with me, and that I was separated from her reality only by my own garbled perception, by my stubborn adherence to how I thought things should be in a house where the owner has died. Or maybe, subconsciously, I just didn't want to share. Whatever the reason, I was determined to rise to a level of awareness that allowed me access to the living world, and I used the only tool with which I was proficient – my imagination.

I closed my eyes and pictured my desk in front of the glass wall. I pictured the piney woods outside swaddled in snow. I thought of how the cold would breathe off the glass like a feathery kiss, just enough to announce the colossal presence of winter. Then I superimposed the image of the baby grand, shiny as a sleek black beetle, over that of the desk with its writer's mess of pens and coffee-ringed papers. I imagined the slick feel of its keys and the deep resonance of its voice. When I opened my eyes, I was in the pretty girl's library. In front of me, the piano gleamed in welcome. There was a fire in the fireplace, and books filled the shelves. Under my feet, the plush hide of the Persian carpet felt a foot thick. I'd made it back up the rabbit hole.

At first, I was just glad to be in a well-appointed house with another person. I hadn't realized until then how lonely and frightened I'd been. I might have been content to wander around the comfortable rooms, to read, and to watch my lovely housemate for years, but the terrible cramping came again, making me moan with need. This time, I fell into an armchair whose buttery soft leather I was unable to appreciate and gasped like a man transfixed on a white-hot lance. The reading lamp above me smothered me with a nauseating pall of light that seemed to drag at my skin. I was dimly aware of the girl standing in the doorway wearing a drawn expression. She could hear me! As she gazed into the room, trying to pinpoint the source of the ghastly sound, I flopped backward in the chair and opened my mouth wide for good howl.

Instead, something like a heart within me, some ghostly organ that hadn't been part of my physical anatomy, began to pump. It hurt like hell, shuddering and throbbing, but it also began to wind in the yellow lamplight like an ectoplasmic winch. Blackness bloomed in the air where the light had been and battened like a fist around the lamp's bulb. A sizzling, ecstatic rush of power that was everything good in life filled me. It was like sexual release, like a hearty meal, like the warmth of a fire on a cold night, like triumph. The light bulb shattered, and pulverized glass showered down on me. The girl screamed, and I began to laugh. I'd found something that eased the agonizing hollow cramp.

I felt an immediate flush of strength. My fingers could read the distressed softness of the leather arm of the chair. I squeezed and saw shallow dimples appear on its surface. I reached out for the little dish of mints on the table beside me and pushed it with my finger. It skated off the table and scattered candy over the carpet. The girl in the doorway had fled; I could hear her in the kitchen talking loud and fast into the phone. *It's Tessa! It's worse than ever! You've got to come.*

Well, I could sympathize with her terror, and I hadn't meant to cause it, but at that moment all I could think of was getting more of what the lamp had given me. I got up and went through the house eating up every light that was turned on. Pop, pop, pop went the bulbs. Showers of glass and sparks marked my progress. The girl, Tessa, shrieked and ran past me like she was on fire, but I barely noticed. I was *feasting*, and it felt momentous. The weird heart in my chest no longer hurt as it pulled in the light; it was running like a smooth hot-rod machine, and I had gained solidity and strength enough to grasp handles and fling open doors and drawers, which I did with abandon.

For a while it was like I was high, speeding and floating on my dead guy's version of endorphins. When I came back to myself a bit, I looked around and saw scattered sheet music and candies, books hurled from the shelves to the floor, cabinet doors and drawers hanging open like shocked mouths, and the crunchy crystal puddles of exploded glass from all the consumed light bulbs. I heard Tessa sobbing in the kitchen. When I went in there, she was crouched down behind the breakfast island with the phone in her fist, a dial tone droning into the sudden silence.

I was sorry, and I wanted to soothe her somehow. I mean, if we were going to share the house, she couldn't go on being afraid of me. I walked around the island toward her, and I stepped in a little fall of glass from the overhead chandelier. I heard the soft crunch under my heel and so did Tessa who jumped as though I'd poked her with a fork. She was looking at the crushed glass and moaning like a woman caught in a nightmare. I glanced down and saw the perfect imprint of my bare foot in the debris. I squatted beside her and tried to whisper a reassurance in her ear, to tell her that I meant no harm, that I came in fucking peace, but the stupid girl shot away from me on her hands and knees and turned at bay in front of the refrigerator. She held her hands splayed out in front of her like a wizard in a kids' movie, and her eyes were big and scared.

"Go away and leave me alone," she yelled.

I made another attempt to talk to her. "Tessa —"

I didn't have a chance to get another word out. She heard her name and rose to her feet in one snake-smooth uncoiling.

"Get out," she screamed. Then a sly look came into her eyes, and in a loud voice - as though I might be deaf as well as dead – she said, "I've called a medium. She'll be here tomorrow morning, so if you don't want your ass exorcised you'd better leave now."

Well, I thought, you inhospitable little minx. But yelling threats at me seemed to have calmed her. I leaned against the island and watched as she tugged her sweater straight (*nice sweater stretching over very nice breasts*) and ran a hand through the sexy tangle of her long ash-blonde hair. A flush of color came back into her face, and I approved the combination of a roses-and-cream complexion with wide aquamarine eyes. A thrill of desire swept through me, not the horrible cramping hunger of before, but the sweet desire of a man for a woman, and I felt myself growing hard. Surprise! I gaped down at the front of my jeans in disbelief. Then I started to laugh. I mean, the situation was ridiculous, and yet I was pleased to find I still had something like a body. Tessa heard the laughter and flounced out of the room in frightened fury.

I let her go, figuring I might try to talk to her again later. For the first time since my death, I was happy. I felt almost alive again, even if I was invisible, and I thought that with time Tessa and I could become friends. I had to chuckle at the thought of the medium coming the next day to banish me, probably to shake bells and feathers, or to smoke me out with smoldering herbs. My own weird existence aside, I'd never believed in all that mumbo jumbo. I thought I might just make myself scarce and let the woman ply her scam on empty air. Still chuckling, I went over to the kitchen door that led to the deck and put my hand on the knob. It was cold and sleek, and I could grip it. With my strange ghost heart pounding, I turned it and opened the door.

I opened the door! A heartbeat later I stood on the snowy deck overlooking the woods. I was outside, pacing the deck in a welter of excitement. I went around to the lake overlook and stared down at my frozen grave. Several crows erupted from the pines, flapping upward like funereal garments torn free from a clothesline, their harsh voices accusatory and somehow mocking. I walked across the snow-covered cedar to the stairs, meaning to go down to the dock, and encountered a thick gluey interface that I was unable to push my way through. It was the same when I attempted to jump from the deck rail. A few light bulbs had not provided enough juice to liberate me from the house, even if I could now open the doors. Disappointed,

I returned to the library and sank into the leather hug of the armchair in front of the fire.

The sun had gone down, and the evening had flown after it like a possessive lover. I must have dozed, if that's possible. When I woke, Tessa had gone to bed, and I was alone with the solemn ticking of the clock on the mantle. I didn't feel well. I was clammy and cold; the lake was coming out of my pores and dripping on the carpet with a metronomic monotony. I could smell its mineral tang, with its unlovely suggestion of dead fish. I rose up in fright and disgust, only to fall back as my heart gave an excruciating lurch. *But that organ burst and rotted long ago.* I looked at the lake water glazing my skin like the slick layer of melt that forms on the spring ice, and I wondered if the thing in my chest was a heart after all.

Only the hallway nightlights were burning as the hunger came back, worse than before. I writhed and gripped the arms of my chair, and the blackness that had earlier reached out for the delicious glow of the lamps began to fill me up, darkening and changing me until I was a huge shadowy version of myself — one with enormous long-fingered hands at the ends of elongated spidery arms. My shoulders hunched and knotted. My jaw broadened and lengthened, bristling with teeth. I had become the personification of my hunger.

The transformation robbed me of my voice, and I could produce only rough, guttural growls. I didn't feel hollow now, but ravenous - a slobbering fiend mad with appetite. The part of me that was Ed Spencer was shoved to a dark corner where it could only watch. I rose like vapor and flew to the wall where I jammed my attenuated fingers in the electrical sockets. The nightlights winked out, the electric clocks ceased their murmurs, and the red eye of the alarm system went dark. Not enough. Like a crust thrown to a starving bear. I snarled and snuffled around for a few minutes, then sped up the stairs and down the short hallway to Tessa's room.

She lay on her back, the quilt kicked away, breathing slowly. Sleep insulated her and kept her from me, safe in her own dreams. A wavering golden light surrounded her, one I hadn't seen before, and the breath grew thick and hot in my throat. A translucent thread of drool ran from my mouth, and I swiped at it with my frightful claw. The light had a fragrance that caused my heart to grind in my chest. I moved closer, sniffing hungrily, until I floated above Tessa's sleeping form. I tried to say her name and only growled, but it was enough. She opened her eyes. My hands fell on her. My jaws stretched wide.

66

It's past midnight now. I'm sitting here in the library, staring out at the dark, windy silhouettes of the pines and the bone-bright gleam of the naked sycamores. They're like monsters, those trees, with their rough shaggy pelts and cold twiggy fingers that reach for you with such wicked stealth. They always unnerved me a little when I was alive, but there are worse kinds of monsters. I'm very strong now. I've been down to the lake, and I could go farther if I liked, but what I really want is to make my way to the city. The city is so full of light.

So, I'm waiting. For the first chill flush of dawn, for the new day that holds such promise. Tessa lies in her bed, empty and cold, staring sightlessly at the ceiling. She's waiting, too, in a way. We're both waiting for the knock on the front door, for the anticipated visitor to enter calling out, *"Is anybody home?"*

She'll find us both at home, although I won't be staying.

The White Duchess

※※※

"**U**pon my return, I was changed. Three days in the cool dark, with the small patter of lizards' feet on the tiles of the roof, like rain. The open grillwork of the windows let in moths at night, like birds with their enormous somber wings, their bodies heavy and indolent. They bumped against the shadows flung by the openhanded candle flames. Those wax goddesses so free with their light, so wanton, yet ever beneath the glory of the sun of whom they are jealous. I like the candles better, now."

"I remember waking, so gradually it was like surfacing through indigo waters. I rose by slow degrees toward the swaying of the palms, whose whispering I could hear high in the air above me. And then I was awake; the clinging fever of darkness vanished, and the sweet pure night pierced me."

My brother and I first saw Lucienne at a salon given by Lady Steuben. We had made port a few days earlier, propelled out of the maw of a storm that had wrung prayers from the captain and crew alike. We were happy to see lights and gaiety. How frightening the sea had been, leaden and unappeasable, and the night like a fist slammed repeatedly against her depthless rage. When I met Lucienne, I thought her eyes were like that night-stunned sea. There was nothing and everything in her gaze. I was reminded of the cold appraisal of a shark.

She gave her hand to Robert and said, "Welcome to our little island, Monsieur. I hope you will be happy among us."

The "White Duchess" was what they called the plantation. Sugar cane ate up the ground in three directions, wealth rolling up to the impenetrable humidity of the forest, and the sea lay heaving to the north. The house was low and sprawling, girt by wide verandas, the tall windows and doors open to catch the sea breeze. When our carriage pulled up on the red dirt drive, we were greeted by the screams of peacocks.

The servants gathered on the veranda. A tall brown man named Arthur handed me from the carriage with a solemn expression. None of them smiled. Robert asked if the foreman were about and Arthur turned and spoke a few curt words. From the shadows at the side of the wide, low stairs a skinny half-naked boy sprang up and ran toward the fields, his bare heels drumming the red earth. Without any more fanfare than that, we entered and took possession of our late uncle's plantation.

The dim, high-ceilinged rooms were filled with shifting light and shadows, and the white scrim of the draperies floated on the constant salt breeze. I went immediately to the room that was to be mine, so exhausted by the relentless heat of the long drive that I cared little for the pleasures of touring our new home. Though the sun had been cruel, the dim gustiness of the room seemed almost chill. The foamy drapes and bed netting billowed and writhed like fog, and I shivered.

I turned to the impassive maid. "Is it customary to keep the house so open? The hallway is positively windy, and this room seems cold."

"The sea breeze is cleansing, Miss Ann. Blows away the sickness, the one took your uncle. Very bad on the island it was, carrying off all sorts of folk, even them that thought they was immune. The sea breeze rides it away."

A curious turn of phrase. I had heard something of the fever that had swept the island – some tropical malaise that rendered its victims weak and delirious, and often carried them off. The few who survived were never strong again. When they passed on, the superstitious islanders drove priest-blessed nails through their eyes and tied stones to their hands and feet before entombing them in niches scratched from the walls of the sea caves. Like an unloved guest, the fever returned from time to time, and so this frightful practice was well established. I did not want to encourage such childish thinking among the servants.

"That was over a year ago, Marie. I think it will be safe to close my bedroom windows."

Marie stared for a moment, her lips trembling on the point of speech, but in the end she crossed to the windows and pulled the shutters close. The restless drapes stilled, the bed ceased to heave like a ship in a storm, the shadows fell senseless into the corners. I waved Marie toward the trunks to be unpacked and collapsed into the embrace of the billowy duvet.

Lucienne Ste. Martin came with the White Duchess, like a minor addendum to the inheritance. Her marriage to Robert would forge an alliance between the plantation and Ste. Martin shipping. It was a business arrangement of some years' negotiation between our uncle and Lucienne's father, Charles Ste. Martin. Robert had first been made aware of the possibility when he finished his university studies. Uncle's letters had been enthusiastic, and then later, cautious. Robert had heard nothing of the match for nearly two years, and had just about decided that the engagement had fallen through when news of Uncle's death reached him, along with confirmation that both his plantation and his bride awaited him.

"Well, I'm to marry a pig in a poke," Robert jested. "Such is the price of riches and adventure. I only hope she has a pretty face."

He was good-natured at the prospect, having formed no attachments at home, and he turned his will to the task of building the family business – a goal much more readily within his grasp were he wedded to the Ste. Martin girl. He was admirably practical. Romance, I fear, is my weakness.

I tousled his hair. "You're the pig in the poke, brother. Do you think a young woman wants to be the pawn of unscrupulous businessmen?"

Lucienne did not seem to mind in the least. She was dark and ethereally beautiful as a fairy tale heroine. She played the piano, danced with grace, and dressed elegantly. The three of us were in constant company at the round of engagement parties thrown by the islanders. Robert was pleased, but I felt uneasy. The girl was charming and lively in conversation, but lapsed almost into torpor when not engaged. I found myself comparing her unfavorably to a wind-up doll I had when a child. Left alone, Lucienne seemed wound down. Unlike my doll, though, there was a disturbing quality of *anticipation* about the girl. A sly, febrile glitter seemed to light her dark eyes, yet never did it achieve the warmth of actual interest. Nor could I find in myself any liking for her family. Rough sailors in silk waistcoats, the lot of them, and steeped in the heathen beliefs of the natives. Lucienne's grandmother, Odette, accompanied her with the inevitability of the tide, and by turns cossetted the girl or thrust her forward like a trained seal.

One night, after supper with the mayor, our party moved to the drawing room for cards and gossip. I watched Lucienne dazzle everyone in turn, bright and spirited on Robert's arm. But when my brother was called away to the study by his fiancé's father to discuss matters of business, the flame that was Lucienne guttered low and acquired that nightmarish lurking quality that so troubled me. Her dour brothers and uncles took no more note of her than of the furniture. They stood in a brooding knot about the fireplace, drinking brandy that should have been consumed at the dining table before they joined the ladies. No such niceties were observed on the island, nor did Gerard Ste. Martin feel ashamed of the brazen and unwelcome appraisal he lavished on me.

The other ladies of the party were embroiled in a game of hearts. Lucienne stood like one asleep by the tall window that overlooked the street, and yet there was a terrible inwardly-turned vivacity about her. I thought she was like the creature some in the islands called "zombie", devoid of any will of her own and only eager for instruction. I became aware of Odette watching me as I watched her granddaughter, and I felt a frisson of guilty fear when our eyes met. Perhaps she guessed at the direction of my thoughts, for she stood and crossed to the window.

"Miss Ann," said the harridan, "does not my pet play sweetly?"

With that, the old woman propelled the girl to the piano where Lucienne was immediately animated by the sudden regard of the ladies, and commenced a lovely air. Her playing was accomplished, yet lacked the verve that pleasure in the music lends.

Odette came to sit beside me on the divan, compelling me to feign a rapt attention to Lucienne's performance. I felt my flesh cringe away from the old woman, an involuntary response of the body that I strove to master. For a long moment she said nothing, only looked at me coolly, as one takes the measure of an opponent. Then she smiled and reached out her slender claw to pat my knee.

"We will have to do something about you, Miss Ann." She showed her yellow teeth at my gasp. "A match, of course, is what I mean. It is time you thought of marriage, and left your brother's house to be mistress of your own."

"I am grateful for this existence. They could have imprisoned me by the sea, my people. They could have made me heavy and inert as a stone, denied me this wild joy. Instead, they sold me, and I will be a bride. I do not mind. I go to my fate compliant as a child, knowing what none of them can know. I am beyond them. Oh, how I have traveled!"

"Three days I lay waiting, rising through the fathoms of darkness. On the third night, I put one bare foot against the stones of the floor. Such a simple act, yet fraught with terror and wonder. After that, the other foot. I stood. I walked. I was graceful as a young vine, and strong. I left my little house and my hard bed, and I walked naked over the path. The forest was incandescent with heat and moonlight. Drums pulsed in the night; my heartbeat was like that, and the determined tread of my feet. I went toward the drums."

The wedding was a modest service held at the White Duchess. The bride was radiant, though earlier I had found her standing listlessly before my vanity table, my hairbrush dangling from her white fingers. It fell to the carpet as I entered, and Lucienne made no move to retrieve it, nor seemed to have noticed its fall.

"My dear, are you well?"

I took her by the arm. She came with me to the chaise and allowed me to push her down upon the tufted satin in a great rustle and froth of wedding silk and lace. She lay like a wax figure in the sheer drape of her veil, the avid eyes like windows onto living night in the stillness of her face. I drew back with the sudden shrinking notion that I looked upon a corpse.

Lucienne stirred sluggishly. "I am well, Ann. I am only a little weak. Did you know I had the fever? Not long before your uncle died, I rallied. I rallied..."

Her soft voice trailed away with the effort of speaking. I had not known, and I was shocked. Perhaps her weakened health accounted for her strangeness, and yet I did not believe it was so. Her eyes pulled at me with dark promise, but I was repelled as by some black void from which could be discerned the scuttling of beetles. Lucienne made an effort and rose upon her elbow, holding out a pale hand to me.

"Help me up, sister," she whispered.

And I helped her, may God forgive me. I helped her to stand and finish dressing, and to walk like a somnambulist to the little chapel by the library. When she saw Robert standing before the priest, waiting for her, her spine stiffened and she bloomed before my eyes. Gone was the wilting rose of a moment before, replaced by laughing health and vitality. She fairly danced to the altar. I should have stopped them, but how? How to tell Robert, wreathed in smiles, that his bride was - what? At the very least, unwell. At worst, monstrous.

In the midst of my indecision, Odette appeared at my elbow, drawing me to the side of the room, her fingers like an icy vise.

"Come, Miss Ann," she murmured, "let an old woman take charge of you. Who knows but that you, too, may be married one day soon?"

And so I stood mute and miserable beside that greedy witch and watched my brother go happily to his doom.

"Night and candles, darkness and flame. They are like music to me! The bridal chambers were filled with them, and the shadows that are their children. The windows were open to the mighty roar of the sea. The fathoms of dark water, the fathoms of night. The palms thrashed the sky and the clouds raced away from their violence. I knew my duty. I was to lie with this man, to be mistress of his house. I could never bear him children, but I could keep him bound...bound...to the sea? No. To my father's ships, lashed tight like a furled sail, and the sugar would make them all rich. Grandmother schooled me. Her tongue is a scourge, her every word writ in flame on the air. She called me back. When the fever took me, she called me back and made me her creature. But she didn't know all. Her ways are not the only ways. And she wasn't there, anyway, to command me in that candlelit room."

"The greater truth is that I belong to the night; it consumed me bite by bite as I journeyed back to the world. It never lets anything go, once caught. I have night in place of blood, a fist of night where my heart once beat, night behind my eyes and right down to the bottom of my soul. I am a doorway into night, and I am glad of it. I can't make you understand the ecstasy or the insatiable hunger of the darkness. When Robert came to me, the night burst into the room - my true husband - and drank him like a fine wine. I drank him. We devoured every spark, the very candle flames were gulped down, and Robert was gone into the depths from which I rose."

"I left the white peignoir upon the bed and wrapped myself in shadows. Like a shadow, I have no home. Yet, like the salt wind, I will find my way in everywhere."

Oh, Robert, my dear brother! I seem to see him in the billowing curves of the drapes, there, and then gone again. His eyes are so sad. Marie assures me it is only the fever, but she makes the sign against ghosts and demons when she thinks I am not looking. She is brave, to tend me so closely, even with the windows open to the stormy howling and surging of the sea that passes for the winter season here. I like the cool of the wind now, and the lash of the rain that dashes in. The sun has forsaken us for weeks; the cane is rotting in the fields. But I am mistress here now, and I try to rise, to see to the crop and the workers dying in their simple homes. Fever. Fever rushes among us like a vampire.

Who is that in the doorway? *Mr. Gerard*, says my faithful Marie. That damned Ste. Martin, leering at me with his feigned concern. I'll never marry him. His family is filling up the house, my house. Get them out! Get them out! Marie tries to soothe me, but I thrash and cry out. Oh, God. I think I'm dying.

No, no, my sweet. That voice, it is rich and dark, I know it. *No,* it says. *You will not die, not really. Only a short rest, and then you will be married. I told you I would take charge of you.*

A fathomless darkness is waiting to swallow me. Odette's face is the last one I see before I drown.

Postprandial

They say I will never be satisfied. Perhaps they are right. They came with smoking torches through the woods, brewing violence, the night I ate the rector. Very put out over that, they were. Well, he was a bony little man, no better than a scrawny chicken. I picked my teeth with his spiny ribs and loped off to lie beneath the wild barberries and watch the blundering hunt. It was cold in the woods, moonless, and a smothering snow dropped in wet, fat flakes. They didn't like it. It hissed on their torches and made their coats heavy. After a few hours, they went home.

A few nights later, I was in the tavern, still in disgrace and with my stomach snarling. None of them would talk to me or stand me a pint. I'm accustomed to such treatment. I sat in the far corner at the barman's left hand and nursed my tankard. The fire smelled like death and roared like a barn ablaze. The sweat started out on my forehead, and I swiped at it, feeling like a devil on a spit. Blind Bob's violin was a torture of clawing nettles inside my skin. I made a noise in my throat halfway between a whine and a growl. Jack, the barman, gave me a disgusted look.

"Get hold of yourself, Davy," he said. "You're in the shit good and deep. Squire's sent for a new parson and the parish is in a godless muddle till he gets here, thanks to you." He swiped viciously with his rag at the puddle of drool before me.

I knew he only meant to advise me for my own good, but Bob's infernal screeching was seven shades of hell, combined with the sensation that I was being boiled alive. Worst of all, I was hungry. I looked out into the night, black as an inkwell and filling up with the whispering snow. This would be my last winter; I knew it sure as I knew my hand before me, squeezing the empty pewter tankard into a crooked, useless lump.

There's no moon in my dreams. I move in its absence like a man. I walk the night road and start at every skreek and rustle like other men. I can feel the panting regard of the forest on me, boring between my shoulders, making me want to turn at bay or run in wild panic. I can feel the soft shiver of the ground under the stalking feet of the predator. I can feel fear. Nightmares, but precious to me. I never asked to be a monster, and until the unfortunate meal of the rector, I kept my hunger away from the village. It means a great deal to be tolerated, to be allowed to walk the streets and take my leisure at the tavern like the rest. They don't have to keep me among them. I know there are some who would put me to death; more now, damn them.

The rector, now, he was of a bloody mind. Always urging them to have my head off, to pin my skin to the wall of the church. Not this skin, weak and naked, but the other. The powerful silver fur I wear sometimes. Oh, it feels so good. You wouldn't think being a beast could be so delicious, but I can tell you that my mind then is clear as a mountain pool and as chilly. Not like the red confusion of my man mind. The rector couldn't understand that I was a victim! I tried to tell him. I was attacked on the night road. I was a man like him, a hard-working man with the dreams and ambitions of a man. He knew me then; how could he turn his back on me now in my despair? Bastard! I'm glad I ate him.

It's an evil moon that rides the winter clouds. It pulls at me like a thousand red-hot hooks. It'll pull my skin off if I'm not careful, and leave only the wolf. I left the tavern and the sullen, moony sheep faces of the villagers. Ran, if I'm to be honest, out into the blessed cold and the frenzied kisses of the swirling snow. Bob's howling violin followed me for a bit, needling my ears and my nerve endings. He's next, the tone-deaf ox. I'll rip his heart out and leave it steaming inside the black hell of his fiddle. Do they think I can't hear them in there, muttering about me? My friends and neighbors. They've been so patient.

Postprandial

They never even spoke of turning me out, even after the incident with the cattle. And the next one, with Abe's coon hounds. And the next one, when little Toby Miller went missing in the blackberry thickets. No. They didn't know about that one, that wicked day. But maybe they suspected. They're so forgiving and compassionate. So docile.

Not the rector, though. He was a hard man, flinty and dried up, with eyes like flaming jack-o-lanterns. I couldn't pass the threshold of his church after my - encounter. It was him kept me out, with his baleful stares and his hatred, though I could smell the fear humming through him like grain alcohol. When I stopped occupying my usual pew, the women of the village became dumb in my presence. Really, what could they say to such a creature, one who would slink from the eyes of God? Bitches! They thought me handsome, once. No, no. I don't blame them. It was all him, the stick in black with his dog's collar. He thought my evil nature prevented me from entering his church. I ate him on his altar, and never was a finer dining table, even if the meal was paltry.

From the hill to the east of the village, I see them gather in the square. Scythes and pitchforks, the damn torches again throwing red light on the snow, and all the leaping shadows make them look like a convocation of demons. The squire rides up with his armed men, their horses snorting steam on the black air. The snow muffles their voices, but I can see what they're up to. My guess is that Jack hadn't liked the look of me as I sat slavering at his bar with my eyes rolling yellow in their bruised sockets. Even a sheep can recognize danger if it's close enough. I have to laugh at them milling about so purposefully, and the laugh turns to a long, deep-throated howl that shocks me, and then delights me. Yes, my last winter, and over sooner than I'd anticipated. I step from the verge of the woods into the cloudy moonlight and let it strip me down to my fur. Perhaps, after tonight, I will finally be satisfied.

The Love Of Gentle Creatures

✤✤✤

The topiary arrived, crated and swathed in burlap, in the rain-slick bed of the Dark's Nursery pickup truck. It was tall enough to rake the overhanging branches of the woodland trees as the truck crept up the gravel drive. Two burly men in flannel shirts and coveralls filled the cab of the truck, the driver's meaty hands dwarfing the steering wheel.

Del stood in the April drizzle beside the clean raked spot where the topiary was to be established. The giants from the nursery rolled creaking from the truck, nodded to Del, and began the back straining labor of lowering the crate to the ground. The thick rope handles groaned, and the men puffed with exertion, their faces red and the brawn of their arms and shoulders threatening to burst their shirt seams. With stoic and stately calm, they eased the crate up to the designated spot and began to dismantle it.

"Ms. Dark said plant it for ya. Sure that's where you want it?" The giant with the shaved head cocked an eyebrow toward the cleared space in the azalea border, just to the right of the front door.

Del, feeling superfluous and somehow irritated by the nurserymen's bovine complacency said, "Yes. That's fine. Can I help?"

Baldy studied him for a moment, the light rain running over his stubbly scalp and down the narrow gullies behind his little pit-bull ears.

"Can if you want. Ms. Dark said we was to do it, though." With that, he lost interest in Del and turned to help his partner pull apart the crate.

Once freed of its wrappings and rough pine cage, the four-foot tall unicorn reared on its delicate cloven feet and pawed the air with spirit. It was clipped from box, its roots carefully wrapped in more burlap, and it was covered over with tight, tiny buds that would yield buttery blooms as spring progressed. A deft hand had trained it. The unicorn was perfectly formed, showing lines as sleek and dainty as those of a deer. It held its head proudly on an arched neck, and its tail – fashioned after the long, tufted whip of a lion – curled up and around like the handle of a teapot. Del thought he could see the tense and quiver of its muscles, the expressive flash of its eye.

The shorn giant stepped back and took it all in. "Now that's a pretty thing," he breathed.

Giant #2, who sported a greasy black ponytail, made a noncommittal grunt and hove to with a spade in the azalea bed. Soon the two of them were babying the topiary into the earth, handling it as if it were their grandmother's good china. They discussed in murmurs such things as positioning, feeding, tamping of earth, and depth of mulching, fussing at and primping the topiary like nervous mothers. Finally, it was done. Ponytail tossed the tools into the back of the truck and climbed into the cab. Baldy turned once more to Del, who was beginning to shiver in his damp sweatshirt.

"That suit ya, Mr. Penny?" Before Del could reply, the man pulled a sheaf of paper from his coverall pocket and offered it up.

"That there's the information on how to care for your topiary, and Ms. Dark's bill. She said if you have questions, just give her a call." He turned to go, and then seemed to remember an important point. "Oh yeah, she said if you think you can't live with it, she'll buy it back. She said give it some time to make itself at home."

The man favored Del with a gold-toothed leer before striding to the truck.

Del wasn't really a gardener. After his wife's death, though, he'd needed a hobby. Something to burn up all the empty time and something that used him up, too. Sleep had not come easy at first. One day Del had looked out at his small yard hemmed about by woods and had gone out to the garage and gotten a shovel. He had dug all day, removing the sod and stacking it by the wood line, and that night he had fallen into bed in his muddy clothes and had slept the sleep of oblivion. The next morning, aching in every joint and muscle fiber, he had driven the five miles to Dark's Nursery and told Nicola Dark what he had done. She had looked at him for several minutes, and uttered the word that had changed Del's life.

"Shrubs."

It was sound advice. He was a novice at growing things, and he needed help with designing the garden, but shrubbery was tough and forgiving. It filled the space quickly, and Nicola helped him choose a nice variety. He had blooms of one kind or another almost all year, and evergreens in winter. He learned about pruning and shearing, laid down a thick aromatic bed of mulch, and got to know his soil. He added bulbs to his repertoire, and some ornamental grasses, but shied away from most flowers. Five years had passed since he demolished the lawn, and his shrub garden was a favorite on the Wickeford Mills garden tour. Best of all, he slept deeply and almost dreamlessly.

Del had convinced himself that loneliness was just a matter of perception. He had few social outlets, preferring to potter in his garden or tramp the Johns Woods with his camera hunting for subjects he would then go home and paint. The canvases stacked up in his attic bedroom, unseen by anyone and forgotten by Del after he finished with them. He didn't get a dog or a cat, as his sister had suggested, because he couldn't face the prospect of its dying someday. He most definitely didn't date, even though he was not yet 45 and had been told he was good-looking. Donna Greenbrier, down at the Millstone Café, had given him the eye so regularly that he stopped having breakfast there. He felt comfortable discussing the safe and soothing topic of shrubbery with Nicola Dark, and he supposed she was as close to a friend as he had. He was grateful for the time she had spent helping him design the garden and for her patient tutoring, and though he had heard that the Dark family had strange blood, he discounted the rumors. Besides, in a place like Wickeford Mills, strange blood was far from unusual.

His shy regard for Nicola was what prompted him to purchase the topiary. On her last visit to his garden, the nursery owner had remarked upon the starkness of his front door.

"Look, Del," she said, "your door is just a big blank spot between the azaleas. It's not even painted."

Del looked with new eyes, and saw that it was so. His door was the steel kind with a little fanlight at the top, and it was the same utilitarian white that it had been when he brought it home from Sheppard's Hardware. On either side of it the azaleas, which were the luscious frothy white of bridal bouquets when in bloom, took on the look of a gap-toothed hedge. Bewildered, he turned to Nicola for advice.

She rummaged in the glove box of her big white truck, her jeans-clad legs hanging from the open door and her booted toes swinging several inches above the ground. With a huff of effort, she righted herself and waved a cardboard tongue at Del. It was a paint chip, and he began to smile at the warm brick red tones he saw there. Nicola folded it so that her favorite was uppermost and handed it to him.

"That's called Barberry. I think it will look great behind those white azaleas. But you still need something special to greet guests." She squinted at the door as though musing over various options, but Del could tell by the mischievous smirk her lips were trying not to make that she already had a plan.

"I know! A topiary. A big one that can really deliver the wow-factor." She turned outrageously innocent cognac-colored eyes on Del. "I just happen to have the very thing. It came in yesterday. *It's a unicorn.*"

The last bit was delivered in a girlish whisper full of excited wonder, and Del laughed aloud. Within the week, his front door was a deep autumn red called Barberry, and the dainty green unicorn stood guard beside it.

Del rarely used the front entrance. It opened onto the crushed stone parking area before his house, an area that seldom saw visitors. Del mostly came and went through the back door that opened onto the garden and the woods beyond, or through the garage door that opened into the kitchen. So he was amused to find himself going out of his way to use the red door, all so that he might stop for a few moments and view the boxwood unicorn that had come to seem like a companion to him. He marveled at its expressive face and ran his fingertips over a slender foreleg, a small heart-shaped hoof split like a deer's foot. He touched the bare fibrous spiral of its horn, and for breathless seconds the topiary ceased to be a thing of twigs and leaves and became a creature of magic. On more than one occasion he found himself talking to it, and though he felt a bit foolish, it was delightful, too. A harmless game.

"You are a handsome little beast," he told it, after several weeks of giddy admiration. "I hope I can do you justice when it's time to prune you."

Del ran his hand over the curve of its neck and the careful waves of its mane. He was afraid to use the shears on such an exquisite specimen, but the box had begun to look the tiniest bit shaggy — as though the unicorn were growing a winter coat instead of shedding it. He resolved to ask Nicola to do the first clipping, and he would watch and learn. He fidgeted with its neat little ears that seemed so alert to his every word, unaware that he was scratching them as though the topiary were a friendly dog.

That night, an enormous moon shone down in a silver deluge. It poured its cool luminosity across Del where he lay sleeping in the overstuffed chair by his bedroom window, his book from earlier splayed across his knee. The light coaxed him to consciousness, and he turned a bleary eye toward the red dial of the alarm clock and saw that midnight had flown and the quiet one o'clock hour approached. Heavy with sleep, he contemplated the merits of shambling to his bed but was revived by a strange sound coming from the parking area below him. He listened with waking auditory senses to the distinct sound of footsteps on the crushed stone. It sounded like several feet, too, and amid the subtle crunch and scuffle he heard soft rhythmic thuds.

Del rolled to his feet and peeked around the frame of the curtainless window. The parking area was lit like a stage by the blazing moon, and he could discern movement. Shadows shivered over the ground, and a new sound came to his ears. *Crunch, crunch, snuffle, snort.* The sounds were gentle and leisurely, not at all like the sounds of a would-be housebreaker. Del pressed his forehead to the glass and peered straight down the front of the house. In the bright moonlight, he saw the sleek rumps and nervous flickering tails of three deer. Surely they weren't chewing on the azaleas. A sizzle of panic burst like a camera flash in Del's mind as he thought of the topiary. How long had they been out there?

Galvanized, Del flew from the room and down the stairs, his bare feet pounding the wooden treads like war drums. He fumbled at the lock on the front door, cursing his clumsiness, and then threw it open with a mighty heave. The moon showed three white tails, like incandescent flags of truce, fleeing into the forest. He staggered onto his front stoop and fell to his knees beside the topiary. He knew the devastation deer could wreak on shrubbery, and as he raised his eyes to the unicorn, his heart was in his mouth.

The topiary sparkled in the hazy moon glow, its shadow looming up the brick wall behind it. It appeared uninjured, and Del's eyes went to the azalea bushes beside it. All was as it should be. Puzzled and relieved, he climbed to his feet and inspected the shrubs further. The mulch had been kicked about a bit and the deep impress of hooves showed here and there, but if anything was changed, it was that the topiary no longer looked shaggy. It was as sleek as if Nicola had come to clip it. Del passed his hands over the unicorn, and then turned to gaze into the woods. He could hardly credit it, but it seemed that the deer had *trimmed* the topiary with their nibbling, and had done a job that would have made any master gardener proud.

The next morning, Nicola arrived with an order of soil acidifier for his azaleas, and Del delivered an excited narrative about the trio of deer he had seen in the night. As he related how the animals had nipped at the topiary with such delicacy and precision, Nicola's face took on an amused expression.

"I know it sounds fantastic," he said. "But you can see for yourself that it's true."

He gestured at the topiary. The unicorn looked especially jaunty to him today, as though preening for his guest. Pride filled his heart, and something more. It was love. Tenderly, he stroked the topiary's verdant hide. Nicola inspected the unicorn with a practiced eye.

"Del, it looks wonderful. It's really settling in nicely here." She patted his chest, just over his heart. "I can see how well you care for it."

"Do you believe me about the deer? Honestly, I didn't imagine it, and I couldn't have clipped it this well by myself."

He didn't know why it was so important that Nicola accept his story, only that he didn't want her to think that he was teasing her with fanciful tales. She was quiet, digging a toe into the mulch bed, and when she looked up at him her face was serious.

"Yes, I believe you."

She looked toward the woods for a long moment, and then back at the topiary before tossing her hair and smiling. "I'd better get on to my other deliveries. I'll see you later."

As she climbed into the high cab of her truck, she paused with one foot on the running board and gazed at him. "Take care, Del," she said.

Del's job in the registration office of the university, across the river in St. John's Port, suited his need for quiet employment and made use of his tidy habits. Del liked organization. His desk was always neat, his forms always properly filed. His office was a small corner nest with a window that looked out on the groomed maintenance lane between Mallory Hall and the campus library. It was a little used thoroughfare, bosky with dogwoods and mountain laurel, and he often ate his lunch there in solitude, seated on a park bench that had been retired from use on the quad.

One day, Del arrived to an unwelcome change in his tranquil routine. He was to have an assistant, a woman named Marla Rance, who proved to be loud and boisterous in volume, dress, and the application of perfume. Her lacquered face with its aggressively red lips shattered the calm décor of his office like a neon bar sign. Del edged around her as she introduced herself with wide sweeps of her bangled arms. He opened the window and, giving Marla a pained smile, rolled his chair as close to the fresh air as possible.

Things did not improve as Marla became a fixture in the reception area. Her every phone call was a shouted skirmish often interspersed with braying laughter. Her desk was a particolored explosion of bobble head dolls and gim-cracks studded with sequins, feathers, and fluttering reflective streamers. It sailed on the industrial mauve carpet like a festive cruise ship amid a wake of overflowing files. The worst of it was that Marla seemed oblivious to Del's cringing avoidance of her space, and to the emphatic boundary of his closed door. At any moment, she might erupt across the threshold bearing a mare's nest of dog-eared papers, or a glittery greeting card requiring Del's signature for an unknown secretary in another department, or a gooey mash of cake from an office party replete with the puddled remains of a birthday candle. Marla had taken an interest in Del, and the force of her notice exhausted and weighed on him.

After two weeks of this onslaught upon his peace of mind, Del made two terrible mistakes. The first happened one morning as he passed Marla's magpie trove, determined to barricade himself in his office. He saw, on the corner of her desk, a new bobble headed creature. It was a white unicorn with a rainbow mane and tail. It wore a little gold bell around its neck, and its head wagged gently at him. Marla was nowhere to be seen. Del glanced about him, and then reached out a finger and gave the toy a gentle tap. It nodded and gyrated, and Del smiled, thinking of his own unicorn. That was how he was caught when Marla arrived, her cloying vanilla musk preceding her. She was delighted to find Del standing in her domain rather than creeping past it like a shadow.

"You like my little unicorn? I just got it."

She moved to stand beside Del, much too close for his comfort. She radi-ated the heat of a furnace, and he could barely breathe inside her sweet cloud of scent. She picked up the unicorn and pressed her cheek to it, then held it up to Del as though for a kiss. He took a stumbling step backward, but Marla was not about to let him escape. She tickled his nose with the thing's fluffy mane.

"I think it likes you," she cooed. "Do men like unicorns as much as we girls do?" She batted her eyes flirtatiously.

Del's head reeled. He wanted only to flee the monstrous woman and, as he eyed the distance to his door, he spoke without thinking.

"Sure, Marla. I have a unicorn topiary."

"Ooooh," she squealed. "I just love those! You'll have to let me come see it sometime."

Panic gave him wings, and Del mumbled an excuse and vaulted for his office, closing the door on the rainbow unicorn whose comical bobbing had become the wild frenzy of possession. Outside his door, Marla chuckled indulgently and went humming to her work.

That night, Del fell asleep on the couch and dreamed that Marla was outside his French doors, dancing the flamenco on the tile patio. *Tap, taptaptap,* went her heels as she whirled toward the doors. She thrust her garish face against the panes and whispered his name. Del woke with a start, his gaze going to the glass doors. For a moment, he thought he saw dark eyes looking in at him and he bolted upright in alarm. Something tapped speedily away, a grey form in the moonless gloom, and he thought it must be a small deer. Whatever it was bounded off through the garden and vanished into the woods. Del slumped back on the couch, already drifting toward sleep again. He didn't recall until morning that the creature's tail had been long and tufted.

Del's second mistake was thinking himself unobserved as he slipped away for lunch on his quiet bench. It was a warm day, and the lulling purr of honeybees in the laurel blossoms filled the air. He had brought a sketchpad with him, and putting his sandwich and apple aside, he began to draw the bees and flowers in soft pencil, using his thumb to smudge in the shadows. So intent on this study was he that he failed to notice Marla's approach until her figure blocked the light. He looked up blinking, and saw her tilting her head this way and that as she stared down at the drawing.

"Hey, you're pretty good."

She was eating a hot dog, and as she bent closer a glob of ketchup fell onto the corner of his page. Marla pulled a crumpled napkin from her pocket and swiped at it.

"Sorry, hon. I didn't know you could draw. Maybe you could do my portrait."

She sat beside him on the bench, chewing with vigor. Del thought he might be in shock. He felt numb and couldn't seem to think of a single cohesive sentence. Silently, he closed the sketchpad and put it aside. He shoved his sandwich and apple back into the brown paper bag he'd brought them in and pushed the whole thing into the adjacent trash receptacle. He tried to move as far from Marla on the bench as possible, but she turned towards him and their knees touched.

"Hey, Del, you know what? I could come over this weekend and you could draw me. I could see your topiary, too. It'll be fun."

Del was separating from his body. "Come over?"

"Yeah, to your place. I know where it is. I drove past it last weekend, but I guess you weren't home. Anyway, I could come over and bring a bottle of wine. It'll do you good to have some company." Marla made a sympathetic face, as though he were a recent widower still in the throes of new grief.

"No." Del shot to his feet. This was a nightmare. He looked around for help and saw no one.

"You've probably got an art studio or something, huh? I can't wait to see *that*. People say I'm artistic, you know."

Marla glanced at the rhinestone encrusted face of her watch and made a little screech of alarm. "Cripes! I've got a dentist appointment in twenty minutes." She bared her teeth at Del. "Do I have anything stuck in my teeth? Never mind, I've got to run."

She stood and poked Del playfully in the ribs. "See ya Saturday, hon."

Del watched her dash from sight, casting aside the ketchup-smeared napkin as she went, and thought that he really didn't feel very well. He trudged over to Marla's litter and delivered it to the trash receptacle on his way back inside Mallory Hall. In his office, he tossed a few files into his brief case and turned out the light. For only the second time in his ten years at the university, Del Penny left early.

He arrived home around one o'clock with thoughts of the leftover meatloaf in his refrigerator keeping companionable company with his rumbling stomach. The sickening paralysis caused by Marla's assault had ebbed away as he crossed the river into Wickeford Mills, and had left him entirely as he followed Route 9 through the Johns Woods to his house. As he eased his little coupe down the gravel lane, he began to feel like a kid on holiday. He would have the rest of the day to himself, and he was happily making plans of how to spend it when he saw that the topiary was gone.

The breath rushed from his lungs, and it seemed there was no more air to breathe. His stomach rolled into a fist. He roared into the garage, carving a fan into the smooth crushed stone, and fell over his own feet getting out of the car.

Regaining momentum, he sprinted to the front door and confirmed that his eyes had not deceived him. The spot where the unicorn had stood was neat and unmolested. It had not been dug from the earth, nor had it been sawed down. Del slapped his forehead and raked a shaking hand through his hair. It couldn't be, and yet it was; the topiary had vanished like a rabbit from a hat.

The snap of a twig and a soft rustle drew his attention to the woods. Something was moving through the laurels there with furtive intent. Still clinging to the thought of a thief, Del ran toward the woods and plunged through the thick understory. Branches clutched and whipped at him, and the stealthy watcher bolted from cover and raced before him. Swiping foliage from his face, Del crashed after it until he saw that it was a deer. It stopped several yards ahead of him, looking back with wide chocolate eyes, and then it huffed and stepped lightly into the shadows and was gone.

Del walked back to his front door with dragging steps, his clean white shirt soiled and torn, and one loafer missing. His hair hung in his eyes. He could barely bring himself to look at the empty spot where the topiary had stood. He forced his gaze there, and shock unhinged his jaw. The spry little unicorn was back, prancing on its tiny feet, arching its neck, and lashing its tufted tail just as before. If Del hadn't known better, he would have said that its eyes sparkled with mischief. He would have said that it was looking at him with pert humor. For several minutes he could do nothing but stare, and then he dropped to his knees in the soft, fragrant mulch and hugged the topiary.

The next morning, a Thursday, Del strode into Mallory Hall bristling with purpose. He would tell Marla that he found her attentions inappropriate and unwelcome. In fact, he would endeavor to rid himself of the assistant he had never wanted or needed. He had heard that Student Aid needed people. He would work out a transfer that would be mutually beneficial. He was ready with his speech as he opened the door to Registration, but the reception area was dim and quiet. A few of the offices that radiated from it had their lights on, but the sleepy early morning calm that he had always loved was unbroken. The reception staff would not arrive for another half hour. Marla's desk sat in the shadowy serenity like a heap of forgotten party favors. Del walked toward it with the caution of a savvy child winding a jack-in-the-box. Marla was not hiding behind either the desk or the bank of file cabinets. She was not lurking in his office, as a quick survey revealed. He began to relax, but as he flipped on his light he saw it.

In the center of his tidy desk was a greeting card sugared with that vile type of glitter that snows all over everything and clings to the hands for days. Beneath it lay a form, creased, coffee-stained, and staple-torn. Del grasped the form by one bent corner and eased it from under the card. A sticky bit of candy adhered to its back, and it exuded an aroma of vanilla musk and stale tobacco. It was a request for medical leave, dated nearly two weeks ago and obviously jostled about in the bottom of Marla's immense handbag ever since. It informed Del that Marla was having oral surgery, and that she would not be back to work until Monday. This was a bit of welcome news, but it was overshadowed by the dread induced by the glitzy card. Del sat at his desk and opened the card with the tip of his letter-opener. A shower of glitter fell to the blotter.

"Dear Del," it read, *"You'll have to get along without me for a couple of days, but try not to miss me too much. Ha Ha. Can't wait to see you Saturday. I'll bring a picnic lunch and the wine. We can make a day of it. See you then! Marla"*

This message was punctuated by smiley face stickers and flower doodles. Del fell back in his chair and spun slowly toward the window. The letter opener was in his hand, and briefly he thought of plunging it into his heart. Once again, Marla had sapped the life force from him, this time by written curse. He wished he could leave early, but he had meetings to attend that would keep him until evening. The lights fluttered on in the reception area as the secretaries filtered in, chattering softly. Del stood. He had to get Marla's phone number and call her. He had to avert the catastrophe of her visit.

By the time Del left the university that night, the moon was rising. He was exhausted. He had not been able to concentrate on his work or on the meetings that had kept him so late. All his thoughts were turned toward the weekend and the imminent destruction of his sanctuary. He had asked every staff member he could find, but no one knew Marla's phone number. Her personnel file offered up only a blank line on the contact information form. She had filled in the address, but he was informed by a secretary in Admissions that Marla had since moved. The woman from Admissions didn't know where, and further inquiries confirmed that no one else knew, either. Marla had become a juggernaut of evil, bearing down upon him with relentless purpose. He rubbed at his red eyes as he approached the steel truss bridge that spanned the Wicke River. Halfway across he drove into a fog, thick but ragged, that filled up the little town of Wickeford Mills and clotted in the dense Johns Woods.

The moonlight poured down through the patches in the fog and lit it with an eerie glow. The edges of things disappeared, and Del found his tires on the soft berm of the road more than once. He wrestled the little car back onto the hardtop. In the hazy beams of his headlights the trees loomed and then vanished, and the road was only a meager square like a doormat before him. Tired and daunted, he soon felt the disorienting power of the fog. It muffled all sound, and the car seemed to float in a fairy tale forest of infinite depth — an older, even wilder incarnation of the Johns Woods. As he coasted around a wide curve, half dreaming, Del saw a figure detach from the gauzy woods and slip into the road. It froze in the glare of his lights, and he saw a brief glint of moonlight on its spiraled horn. With a cry of alarm, he twisted the wheel and the car left the hardtop with a squeal. The roadside ditch swallowed it with a shuddering crunch, and Del closed his eyes as the rear tires chewed at the air.

Someone was swabbing his face with a piece of velvet. Del looked up through the open driver's side window and saw stars in the liquid night. No. They were eyes he was looking into, dark and luminous. The velvet cloth was a muzzle, now pressed to his forehead in silent acknowledgement of his awareness. A soft puff of warm breath tickled over his face, and then the unicorn was gone. Del released himself from the seat belt, and climbed out through the window into the soothing damp of the fog. The car lay on its side, its grill tilted down, in the ditch. The headlights illuminated the brackish water at its bottom. Del sat on the canted car for a moment, and then hopped onto the berm of the road.

Soft tapping footfalls came toward him, and the unicorn stood quivering in the forest hush. A little further down the road, Del saw two deer tiptoe into the trees. The unicorn pranced in place, and then turned to follow them. Del took a few tottering steps after it, one hand extended in supplication.

"Please." He hitched a sobbing breath.

At the tree line, the unicorn hesitated. It pawed at the short grass, and shook its mane. Its lion's tail lashed the fog. Finally, it looked back and whickered tenderly. Without a second thought, Del kicked off his shoes and followed barefooted into the endless forest.

The Masque At Marzipan

~~~

They went to Marzipan for Halloween.

Imagine it: the wide glass doors open in gracious invitation, every window alight, the fire in the entry hall roaring and bucking up the chimney, the marble floor awash with scampering leaves from the gathered oaks. Without, the wild tossing of the forest in the autumn wind and the frisking shadows chasing away the dregs of mundane day. Within, the lavish expenditure of candles, their glimmer caught and fractured by the thousands of crystals that drip from chandeliers and sconces, and the devilish dark beauty of violins. Marzipan has always been a night place. It is drowsy and petulant in the heat of the sun, shuttered and dim inside, exhausted. The night brings it to life; it rises up and dances, puts on rouge and scent, gets up to all kinds of mischief – mostly of the charming sort. But sometimes it can be cruel.

Anyway, they went there for the annual masked ball – Victoire, Armand, Rene, and Guy. Chic and beautiful, costumed in gorgeous silks and velvets, and the masks! Victoire had diamonds at the corners of her eyes, glistening like tears, and white peacock feathers in her dark red hair. Rene placed the embossed invitations on the doorman's silver tray, returned the man's deep bow with a slight inclination of his sleek and handsome head, and waltzed Victoire into the blazing ballroom.

Have you ever seen the ballroom at Marzipan? Oh, ma cherie, it is a fantasy! The floor is gleaming onyx – to step on it is to glide out upon a glassy sea of

93

night, and all the dancers are reflected there like ghosts or whirling galaxies of muted color. The walls are painted like a forest, filled with nymphs and satyrs, rather naughty but...stimulating. The trees of this forest soar to the jewel box of the ceiling, where the sky is perpetual twilight and the stars are winking gems. Angels and devils fly there, watching the dance below and sometimes engaging in celestial congress. The painting has been remarked on many times, so realistic, so rich with depth and movement. It is of the sensualist school of art, have you heard of it? The artist is, of course, long dead of absinthe poisoning.

So, there were the friends at the ball, in that glorious room filled with music and the heat of revolving bodies, each of the lovely young men taking a turn with Victoire in his arms, bending to kiss her long white neck, to feel the silken brush of her coiffure against his cheek. First Armand, tall and straight as a soldier, then Rene sleek as a cat, then Guy who was shy and stooped a little. The men began teasingly, but Victoire was intoxicating. She was like a fever. Soon they grew bolder, clasping her to them, nibbling at her ears, stroking her bare shoulders. In each of them, a drum began to beat.

Victoire laughed and flashed her dark eyes, flirted and invited, reveling in her own satin skin and in the sensation of strong arms spinning her, the delicious feeling of falling away from the constraints of the day. She was anonymous here, as were her young men, and the air vibrated with possibility. She was flushed, heated from dancing and from her bawdy thoughts. Victoire felt the heat of her body as a shiver at her secret core that radiated out to pink her flesh and make the pulse in her throat jump. Her corset was too tight, and yet her bondage only made her shiver more.

You know what Halloween is, don't you? A door. It is as simple as that. Halloween is a door in the darkness, one not easily discerned as we pass along the corridor of the year. It is a duskiness in the lengthening October shadows. We can step through without realizing it, and others can enter our safe house from the wilds beyond its threshold. That ballroom at Marzipan is a door, too. You probably anticipate what I have to say. Naturally, our friends tumbled through it, and now there are three more lustful satyrs and one more succulent nymph in the masterwork of the mural. That is part of the wicked fun of Marzipan. I don't know if there are ever regrets.

Big Bad Wolf

S he had not been his first choice. He had a curvy little blonde all picked out, and was just unbending from his crouch behind the laurels when a man, equally blonde and like enough to the girl to be her brother, sauntered up the trail toward her. The two had laughed together and gone bouncing off toward the ranger's station, leaving him in the cold woods to fume. Broken plans irritated him. He had made an effort to get his mind right again, pushing his anger to the dark area of his brain where it prowled like a caged cat, and sank back into watchfulness. The sky was full of unreleased snow; he could smell it. His skin brushed up against the dry winter air with an electric crackle that goaded his need. The next one, he promised himself, and it didn't matter what she looked like...

And there she came, swinging down the trail alone with the hood of her fleecy coat pulled up, a long striped scarf wrapped almost up to her nose. She was small and slim as a young girl, and he liked her walk. It was smooth and springy, the stride confident – an experienced hiker with a destination in mind. He waited until she chose the most difficult of the three trails, the one that ran deep into the miles of forest and wound up into the lonely boulder strewn wilds where the rangers seldom patrolled, and then he followed.

The park was vast and had its dangers. There were bears and bobcats. He had heard rumors of wolves, which made him smirk. There was only one hungry wolf in these woods, and he wore it; he flexed his muscles inside the khaki parka, imagining he could feel the tattoo stretch into a lope across the broad plain of his shoulders. If he were forced to be honest, he was nervous about meeting a bear. He hated anything bigger or stronger than he, hated the almost-alien touch of fear.

The woods had an evil reputation. Every year, there were hikers who vanished without leaving behind as much as a boot print. Last Christmas, two women had been found mangled in the brush, igniting the old Sasquatch stories and Indian legends that sold rounds of beer at the LakeShore Inn and guns at the Owl's Eye Trading Post. The deaths had occurred several months apart, in different areas of the park. The rangers had labeled them bear attacks, and he agreed that the first killing might have been done by a bear.

The memory of his last hunt made him grin, a leering exposure of teeth that held no warmth. Almost a full year had limped past since then, and his blood was up. He could be cautious when he had to be. His job in the kayak rental shack provided ample opportunity to target prey, and the fantasy of hunting had been enough for a while, but the work was seasonal. He'd been sitting alone in his two-room cabin for weeks, growing restless. The imminent snow had finally decided him. He wanted to get in one good hunt before the white came down, while the ground was bare and iron hard.

The girl in the striped scarf covered ground in a fast, loose stride that surprised him. He had to work to keep up while maintaining enough distance and cover to prevent her from noticing him. His breath chuffed out with delight. He'd picked a good one; she'd be challenging to trail, though in the end it would be too easy. He watched her skinny little ass in the faded jeans. *Chase me, chase me.* Her narrow shoulders moved in an easy, arrogant swing that he found maddening and ridiculous. What did she have to be so cocky about? He would tower a foot over her, outweigh her by more than a hundred pounds. He'd take the sass out of her one-handed. That was a promise.

They moved through air as cold and grey as any ghost, up the rough trail called Medicine Wheel that ended in a natural clearing ringed with lichen-furred slabs of native limestone. The stone pushed up out of the shaley earth like the great grinding molars of giants. That was the medicine wheel the trail sign referred to; not a tribal artifact at all, but the chthonic jut of the land itself in its eerily purposeful pattern. It was not a place he visited often. His prey invariably chose the gentler trails, heading outward from the hub of the main ranger station towards the sunny deer-peopled meadows, or through the hardwood with binoculars and birders' field guides. He had never dogged anyone up into the hard bones of the mountain where the spruces birthed a land of shadows; where the stones were said to be able to rise and walk, and where winter was a sentient force.

The girl glided upward, slipping like a shadow herself between the conifer boughs that encroached on the trail. She did not pause for breath. She did not look about. She did not hesitate or flinch when his foot struck a stone, kicking it onto the trail with a careless clatter that caused him to bite off a curse. Her lack of nervousness, or even simple curiosity, intrigued and angered him. Didn't she know there were monsters out here? He made the horrible grinning face that was little more than a baring of his teeth. Emboldened, he stepped out of the thick cover of the trees and followed along behind the girl, his boots all but silent on the trail. They approached the medicine wheel, and his hands twitched once, then flexed powerfully. The first snowflakes whirled with lazy grace from the low sky.

The girl stepped into the bare circle and unwound her scarf, letting it fall to the ground. She pushed back her hood and long dark hair lifted into the breeze. He was surprised to see that it was streaked with white. He entered the clearing, thinking of himself as inevitable, a juggernaut of death hurtling toward the spark of her life like a great black wind. The chase was over. He felt almost tender toward her as he stood blocking the trail, and removed his gloves. When she turned toward him, he saw that she was older than he had thought. Her serious urchin's face was unlined, but her eyes were old, impassive as cave-darkness. An electric snap of something almost-alien shot through his veins, but he was already moving toward her before he recognized it as fear. Too late, he saw her change.

The snow fell thick and fast through still air, bringing with it a profound hush. It settled on his face, kissed his open eyes, melted into crimson slush around him where his blood pumped, slower now, onto the stony ground. His thoughts collided and dissipated before he could grasp them. He had a memory of being in the woods tacked to the crumbling wall of his mind like an old and tattered movie poster. The trees leaned into the dark halo of his vision like funeral attendees poring over a coffin. He thought he heard the first rising note of a song, perhaps a Christmas carol. But there were no carolers in the woods. As he dwindled further, shutting down to a single point of light, the song suddenly made sense, and his cold lips spasmed into his characteristic grin. More than one, after all. More than one hungry wolf in these woods.

The Enchanted Lock

What is a woman's hair but the silken fountain of her feminine powers, the repository of magic as old as the moon and tides? Madame Babatskaya smiled a smile so tiny it merely tightened the painted vermilion bow of her lips and imperceptibly flexed the corners of her mouth without disturbing her powdered wrinkles. She stroked the shining darkness of the Lady Annalisa's hair as it slid along the pearly sheen of the girl's chemise. The young noblewoman's every memory, talent, desire, and secret revealed itself to Madame's ancient, knowing hand. Annalisa's hair was a crackling net of unbridled arcane force, yet it kept nothing from Madame as she swept it into a loose chignon, extracting several long sparking threads which she pocketed.

Annalisa shifted her slender weight from one bare foot to the other and regarded her reflection in Madame's mirror. She stood atop a cold plinth of marble, the object of every eye in the room. She was being fitted for her coming-out gown, and Madame's seamstresses studied her as assiduously as portrait artists might study their subjects' outward appearance - the pale swanlike neck and winged shoulder blades, the long milky limbs that seemed to capture the light like fine china, the small breasts like firm young pears fearlessly pressed against the thin silk. The girl was nothing more to them than an assemblage of parts diversely lit - a living geometry more or less symmetrical, of varying degrees of grace or awkwardness. They would use their considerable skills to improve the former and disguise the latter. When they were finished with Annalisa, she would float - a veritable goddess — upon the perilous sea of the Winter Ball.

But first, Madame, with the impeccable *savoir-faire* of a maven of form and fabric, took stock of Annalisa in order to design the only possible gown for the girl - the only gown that Annalisa could wear to the Ball with an utter assurance of victory on that night of nights (for every noblewoman knows the Winter Ball is a marriage market, a whirling waltz of contrived romance and financial intrigue that puts to shame the political machinations of the Palace). Madame turned the girl this way and that, garlanded the nubile form with measuring tape and swathed it in rough muslin bristling with pins like the pale hide of a hedgehog. She stood back from her model and conferred, behind a bejeweled and gnarled hand, with the senior seamstress. She tugged Annalisa's arms straight; tapped her, with an ivory handled walking stick, into erect and straining excellence of posture; and then pinched her to make her relax and look graceful. Marvelous fabrics of every color and texture exploded in the room like fireworks and were tried against the succulent cream of the Lady's flesh. With a flurry of quick, bold strokes, Madame sketched her design, the lines aglow like firelit gold on the translucent paper before they faded to the utilitarian lead of pencil markings.

When Madame had her fill of examining Annalisa, she waved her hand and the shop girls trundled briskly forward with the tea table, setting it between the ivory satin settees in the adjoining parlor. Annalisa was dragged from her pedestal and stuffed into her own clothing before the steam from the spout of the pot had time to curl twice upon the air. The sparkling light and pleasant bustle of the fitting room receded like a fleeing tide, leaving behind dimness and silence, and the girl looked about in bewilderment as she was ushered to a seat opposite Madame. A door somewhere clapped shut, and of the gabble of needlewomen, only the old dressmaker remained.

"Strong tea with much honey is the antidote for winter," purred Madame as she poured and stirred. She handed the young noblewoman a porcelain cup so fine and translucent it might have been a wafer of moonlight. As the girl accepted it, Madame roguishly spiked it with plum brandy. "Mustn't take chill, my dear. I see the snow is falling thick, and the night arrives."

Indeed, the great bow window, so recently gilded by pale winter sunlight, was now glamorous with revolving sequins of twilight snow. Madame snapped her fingers; an unseen attendant struck a match in the purple gloom, and the fire vaulted up the chimney with a gusty roar before settling hungrily upon the snapping apple logs. Annalisa gave a tiny shriek and spilled tea into her saucer. More than a little frightened of the eccentric couturiere, she thought that Madame Babatskaya was like a black and undulating snake with her gaunt grace and her towering onyx hair that, being colored by art rather than nature, reflected no light and only absorbed it.

Madame, her face an eyeless mask in the dancing firelight, presented an eldritch Eastern impassivity, a formidable fusion part Black Madonna, part Baba Yaga. She sipped and sipped her tea, the fiery diamond that adorned her crooked pinkie transcribing arabesques of prismatic brilliance on the air. She stared at her companion until Annalisa's cup chattered against the saucer and the girl felt quite faint with nervous tension. The fire was all the light in the darkening room, and endowed a weird liveliness upon the shadows that hovered near, touching, stroking, advancing their thin fingers toward the lemon cookies, hanging about Madame in a whispering clutch like back stair gossips. As the first star ignited in the fathomless blue of the evening, the lamps glowed up with sudden gaiety, a starched maid appeared and whisked away the tea things, and the tenebrous brood receded to their rightful places among the drapery folds and deepest corners of the room. The heavy atmosphere puffed away on the tinkling exhalation of the mantle clock and, if Madame did not look precisely commonplace, her smile was warm and comforting.

"My dear gurrl," she said, "I perceive that the Ball causes you much anxiety, and not the usual excited tremors of a flower of the nobility. Do you not wish to find a rich and handsome husband there?" Madame, who remembered her own long-ago marriage with raffish pleasure, cast a sly, glittering look at the blushing Annalisa.

"Oh, Madame, I do not. I cannot avoid being displayed there like a mare at the Beast Market, but I will refuse all offers, I swear it!" Annalisa burst into hot tears and covered her face in her hands.

Madame withdrew the dozen strands of Annalisa's hair from her voluminous pocket and began to plait them into a ribbon as slender as hope. Her skeletal fingers found no difficulty in this, though it was akin to braiding spider's silk. They flew unheeded at the task as Madame regarded the angry, weeping girl.

"Perhaps it is a particular suitor you mean to cut? Count Hollen is favored by your parents. He is a wealthy and powerful man, though his reputation is... unsavory."

Madame wrinkled her nose, as if at a bad odor. If these elite, nonsensical creatures would persist in selling their daughters to satyrs, they could expect to be repaid by the girls with nothing less than horror and disobedience. Madame was much in demand to dress the young sacrifices, and most went willingly enough to be displayed like bloody steaks before hungry wolves, but she did not approve of the Ball or of its mercenary atmosphere. This girl before her could, perhaps, be saved if she had courage and determination.

Madame made her decision. "I know your heart, my dear. It cleaves to another already, but your beloved cannot compete with the fortune and position of the Count. Will you persist in this infatuation?"

Annalisa only wept harder. "I would run away if I could. My dear George is a fine and honest man. What do I care for heaps of ancient money or cold social standing? It cannot give me love. But I am a prisoner in my mother's house."

She slumped down upon the carpet, her head pillowed in her damp sleeves, and bawled. Madame leaned forward and lashed her smartly across the bare nape of her neck with the finished plait of hair. Stung, Annalisa bolted upright, her nostrils flaring in outrage, and spoke a word that would have shocked and dismayed her governess.

Madame permitted herself a brief chuckle. "I am happy to see some spirit, Anna. You will need all of it and more if I am to help you."

The dress shop was in an uproar. Astonished seamstresses chattered in a babel of languages, laughingly scandalized, as they raced about drawing and cutting patterns, flinging silks and velvets at the dress forms, wondering at Madame's bold departure from tradition. Early this morning, she had returned from a secret fitting (the senior seamstress whispered to the senior embroiderer that Madame had gone to a gentleman's rooms in the fashionable White Garden district, and absolutely unattended!) and announced that they would be creating an evening suit for a gentleman attending the Winter Ball. They had screamed at the daring of it. The men of Tailor's Row would curse them; there would be a barrage of hot language between Monsieur Aristide and Madame that might even come to blows (their money was on Madame as the victor in that particular *combat domaine*), and the face of couture in the City would be changed forever. Madame, impervious to the flap she had caused, gave out the suit's measurements, narrow and long, but put them to work first on the audacious gown she had designed for the Lady Annalisa. Good God, as if one outrage weren't enough! Spirits were high as Madame retired to her private office, ostensibly to design the incendiary suit.

In the quiet of her office, Madame let down the lofty nest of her hair one long looping tress at a time. She searched the inky mass of it like a woman rummaging in a trunk, examining and discarding curl after curl until it hung about her like a sooty curtain. At last, near the center of the dismantled tower, she found the lock she sought and untwisted it. Like the rest, it was the flat, emphatic color of coal. Madame sighed, and with no more ado than if she were ripping out a crooked seam, she took up her shears and snipped it off close to the scalp. Immediately, it began to grow again, and Madame, laying the cut lock aside with care, reversed the process of letting down her hair.

She took the yard-long tress to her washstand and dipped it in the basin, lathered it gently with fine goat's milk soap, and rinsed it. A black slick bloomed on the water as the dye came away, and left the hair in its natural glory. Madame laid it on a towel, blotted it dry, and looked upon the miracle of her own feminine power. The hair was still black, but now it gleamed and pulsed with iridescence, flashing deepest blue and purple like glints of night. Stripped of its disguise, it caught and bent the light into dark rainbows, smoked with sultry shadow, recalled the sheen of a sun struck raven, whispered sorcerous promises. To touch it would have been to stroke the liquid hide of Lethe, to drowse in the concupiscent eddies of the besotted senses.

Madame carried it to the small loom that stood in an alcove of its own with shuttered doors to close it away from prying eyes. On the loom was started a bit of black gauziness, fine as breath and shimmery as a winter night filled with black stars. Into this, Madame wove the darkly blazing lock of her hair and the insubstantial plait of Annalisa's hair. A shadow could not have been sheerer. When it was complete, Madame removed it from the loom. It wafted up on the unfelt currents of the air and danced there for a moment like smoke before being gathered gently and placed in a hatbox on the work table. She would cut it and sew it herself when the time came. Satisfied, she sat down to design a man's suit.

The night of the Winter Ball was clear and cold as the pristine pane of ice on the river that undulated at the feet of the Palace. Snow had fallen all the day in thick tufts like swans down, and the city was plush and sleepy under the soft mantle of it, but now only the finest and most dazzling of flakes sailed from the cloudless obsidian vault of the sky. These ephemeral flakes whirled down like diamond dust, hard and sharp, and stung the skin with their fleeting kisses. As the Palace began to glow with light from every window, the shimmering sift of this snow cast a glaze upon the mounded fluff from earlier in the day, so that every flicker of the street lamps was replicated in bright kaleidoscopic smears. The blazing Palace gleamed up from the smooth white ground before it, and from the more precise mirror of the frozen river, until it seemed to float on a sea of kindled crystal and fiery gems.

For a short time the city appeared as though suspended in an enchantment, everything still and silent as a held breath, trembling on the precipitous edge of the glittering night. And then, the spell was broken by the first merry jingle of sleigh bells, by the susurrus dash of the runners over the virgin snow, and by the laughter and high spirits of the rosy cheeked parties speeding their way to the Ball, tucked beneath mounds of fur rugs. The carriage lamps, nodding from limber poles that arced above the open sleighs, set awhirl the motionless luminosity reflected on the ice. The Palace doors flung wide their arms, and the first sweet strains of the Imperial Orchestra drifted onto the night air. The Winter Ball had commenced.

Inside, the Palace was golden and magical with shattered light from a thousand crystal-bedecked chandeliers and candelabra. A herald in officious scarlet livery declared with bombastic fervor the names and titles of those who entered, first blaring upon a trumpet and then shouting in a voice of thunder. Count Hollen arrived alone and paced with sober majesty through the wide entry hall with his white fox cloak swirling about him like snowfall, causing a scurrying of whispers as he posed on the top of the wide stair above the ballroom. With a flourish, he shed the cloak and dropped it into the quick hands of an alert footman.

If he was not young, he was still in his prime, and cut a dashing figure in his ivory and gold evening dress and lavender gloves. If he preened like a peacock before the hens, he had fabulous wealth to justify his vanity, proven by the coy flash of diamonds at his cuffs. If his lip curled cruelly and his eyes were cold, his position and power were unassailable and weighty as a royal mantle. Though few of the young women assembled were unconscious of a frisson of fear in his presence (his wicked reputation having preceded him), still they twittered and fluttered about him as he descended the stair. For his part, the Count took their adulation as his due, with courtly grace and a touch of ennui. There was but one unplucked rose of interest to him this night, for Count Hollen had determined finally to marry. He cast his jaded gaze about for a glimpse of Annalisa.

Next to arrive was George, Lord Eastmarch, whose remote border province had nothing to recommend it but its great beauty and clean air. The assembly turned away with polite boredom, uninterested in the Marcher lord's wholesome and homely domain of farming, forestry, and hunting. George's handsome, smiling face betrayed no hurt. He had come to the Ball with a single burning purpose, and he paused only briefly atop the stair, sweeping the ballroom with a keen eye. He stood broad-shouldered and lean among his friends from the University, who jostled about him in a good-natured throng. Mere students, be they ever so noble, failed to impress the herald who sniffed, expelled a dismal *blat* from his trumpet, and mumbled over their names so that no one in the room took any notice.

The young men galloped laughing down the stairs in a knot of long limbs and dark jackets, intent on the destruction of the immense buffet and the quaffing of many bowls of sparkling punch. George was anonymous among them, and so his black evening suit was unremarked by the crowd, who would have been astonished at its lustre, by the intricate embroidery that richened it with jetty stylized feathers visible only when they caught the gleam of the candlelight, and by the cut that fit him like a skin and made of him a sleek, manly shadow. As he turned aside from his fellow students, the fractured gleam from a crystal candelabrum picked out the gorgeous needlework wings on the back of his jacket, and struck dark fire from several threads of more than usual glossiness. Threads that flickered purple and indigo, and released a subtle shadowy smoke that clung about George's shoulders, close and fine enough to make the eye uncertain.

As he surveyed the crowded room, George thought he saw Madame Babatskaya gliding along its perimeter. Thinking to ask after Annalisa, he moved toward the tall regal figure, but halted in confusion when the woman turned toward him. It was not Madame after all, but a much younger woman, her face as lovely and pitiless as that of a carved goddess. Her hair was piled high and loose, with long flashing curls like shards of night allowed to cascade from a sumptuously jeweled and old-fashioned tiara. Her lance-thin body was sheathed in an antique gown of darkest red. Perhaps she would have seemed eccentric, or been sniggered over behind fashionable hands, if she had not carried herself with the gravity of a queen. Instead, the chattering crush grew subdued and parted for her with deference as she passed, and began their noise and gaiety again when she paced on. The bewildering woman came close to George, her fathomless eyes falling down the length of him, before looking him full in the face and tipping him a slow wink.

The herald's trumpet blasted a sudden fanfare. His voice boomed out the names of the Lady Annalisa and her noble mother. The reveling host turned to see, and George caught his breath at the sight of his beloved. For an eternal moment the room was as still and silent as a gallery of statues, and then a hubbub of excited conversation broke like a wave. Annalisa descended the stair in her tight-fitting gown of watered silk, black as mourning in a room of whipped pastels and virginal white. The corset-like bodice pressed upward the pale mounds of her breasts, and her flesh was snow against night. Long supple black gloves stitched with stylized jet feathers rose high above her elbows. A tall sheer collar, shot through with sparking threads that twisted the light into dark rainbows, framed her neck and shoulders and fell to diaphanous smoking ribbons that trailed behind her. Beside her, Annalisa's mother moved with stiff mincing steps, her face an angry mask. Clearly, she was displeased with her daughter's gown, but the thin slash of her lips creaked upward when she saw Count Hollen waiting at the bottom of the staircase. Taking one of Annalisa's dark-clad hands in hers, she set it in the grasp of the Count and watched him bend over it before whirling Annalisa away in a waltz.

The night flew on, the candles wilted and wept wax upon the opulent buffet tables, the couples whirled like autumn leaves across the flawless ice of the marble floor. Parents watched their opportunities and negotiated desirable engagements for their offspring. The haggling was in full roar, accompanied by much changing of partners and petulant tears behind the velvet draperies. Some contestants became drunk with too much punch, too much dancing, too much intoxicating winter night, and were carted off to quieter salons to be fanned and chafed into recovery. As the great gold-chased clock by the balcony doors called out a quarter to midnight, Count Hollen handed Annalisa to a young dandy in pistachio green and settled comfortably beside the girl's mother on a quilted velvet settee. It was time to reach an accord in proper contractual form, and in deference to his maturity and dignity, he could dance no more. Enflamed and flushed, with the slender imprint of Annalisa's young body burning upon his where he had pressed her indecently close all the evening, the Count drained a cup of punch and turned his leering, jack-o-lantern face to the matron beside him. *Still a damn handsome woman,* he thought and slid a bit closer, the better to whisper in her ear.

George stood in front of the balcony doors, feeling the faint breath of cold from the glass against his back. All the evening he had watched Annalisa dance with the Count, her sweet face blank and resigned, her feet moving her like an automaton about the ballroom. The wolfish Count had clasped her to him and breathed over her neck and shoulders, fogging her diamonds and almost slavering, and the muscle in George's jaw twitched with rage. When he thought the sight unbearable, when he felt he must challenge the monster or go mad, he had caught sight of the dark, queenly figure in the antique garnet gown watching him. Almost imperceptibly, the woman shook her head. With a crook of one fine eyebrow, she had motioned George toward the balcony, and then glided to stand before the enormous clock. He had hesitated, but had seen Count Hollen collapse red-faced upon a settee and begin to guzzle punch. Annalisa whirled on, now held with proper formality in the arms of an unknown young man. Relieved, George had made his way around the ballroom.

The cold at his back felt fresh and clean, and he was tempted to fling open the glass doors and let the night into the room. The heat of the revolving bodies and the smothering scent of the candlewax were claustrophobic. He looked down at his fantastic evening clothes and felt a fool. A suit of embroidered feathers was not the answer to his problem. How could he ever have believed it? He wished for his pistol, for his hounds, even for the chance to use his hard fists. They clenched as he thought of smashing the smug jaw of Count Hollen, but a cool touch, light as a spider, brought him back to himself. The woman in red stood before the clock, close enough to touch, and her enigmatic face gave him a chill. It was a face he knew, and yet it was that of a stranger.

"Madame?" He cleared his throat and shuffled his feet in embarrassment. "Forgive me; I thought I knew you--"

He stopped again, and then rushed on. "Madame, is it really you?"

The woman did not answer, but her full red lips quivered infinitesimally as though they would smile. Instead she turned her eyes to the clock's ornate face. Reaching up to her fiery tiara, she grasped one of the gems there and drew forth a long shining pin. The wicked silver length of it caught a gleam of light as she held it poised for the space of a breath, and then she plunged it into the filigree of the clock's hands upon the instant it struck midnight, skewering them in place. The clock began to toll the twelve sonorous notes of the hour, but its voice was slow and labored. All sound and motion in the ballroom slowed. Across the room, Count Hollen tilted languidly forward, his chest heaving like a dilatory bellows as he laughed into his partner's décolleté. His hand grasped her thigh and squeezed so lazily that George could watch each crushing wrinkle of her gown forming. The orbiting dancers drifted past like people in a dream, and the woman he believed, against all reason, to be Madame Babatskaya reached out a long white hand and effortlessly plucked Annalisa from the waltz.

Freed from the spell, the girl stumbled and caught herself, staring at the strange woman with frightened eyes before catching sight of George. At once, Annalisa flew to his arms with such exuberance that he staggered backward, bumping the handles of the glass balcony doors. They flung open, and the young couple stood upon the threshold bathed in the refreshing cold and a swirl of scintillating snow dust. The bewitched clock growled out the sixth note of midnight, and the sorceress in the red gown stepped forward. She reached into her reticule and drew forth a handful of shimmering black feathers.

"Fly with your bride, my lord," she said. And to Annalisa, "You are free now, child."

Pursing her lips as for a kiss, she blew the feathers from her palm. They spiraled together with the snow on the cold air. Annalisa and George watched as the feathers fell toward them. At their touch, the black suit and gown with their magical threads of hair and clever embroidery granted them flight. With a joyous clap of wings, two ravens rose from the balcony. They circled the palace towers, and as the clock struggled to voice the seventh note, they turned east toward the Marches.

Through the snowy midnight streets, a canopied sleigh drew Madame Babatskaya and her maid toward home. Agnes slumped blearily in a corner, muffled by fur rugs with her feet on a hot brick. It had been a long evening of waiting for her mistress in the ladies' salon, and she was that done in, she was. Across from her, erect as a maypole, Madame lifted a silver flask to her crimson lips and sipped. Good plum brandy, fire for a cold night. Agnes stifled a yawn behind her hand, and Madame's dark eyes fell upon her.

"Agnes, my dear, did you not tell me that Count Hollen has given up his tailor?"

"Aye, Madame. The Count as near strangled the man for botching the cut of a morning suit. Monsieur Aristide has presented his card and hopes to take his place." Suddenly suspicious, Agnes narrowed her eyes. "What are you thinking, Madame?"

But Madame Babatskaya did not answer. She only pinched her lips in her taut little smile and wondered what Monsieur Aristide would say to losing another client.

The Boarder

One November day, he was simply knit to the twilight, a darker than grey slub in the scarf of burgeoning night and hesitant snow. It was cold. The clack of the sign in the wind was a bone on bone percussive, flat and dismal — Room for Rent. His breath was a ghost leading a gaunt shell by a vaporous chain over the bare, crackling boards of the porch. Lean and worn, his face a wicked wedge of sharp shadows and burning eyes, Mephistophelian insolence and a slight limp marked him a dark angel or traveling god, a tramp, a thief, a simmering violence, and skittish about a room with a closed door — yet, cold and hunger and deep weariness drove him in, and he circled the furniture with suspicion.

We eyed each other, did not extend friendship but condescended to shelter together. It was night now and howling, and the kitchen was a neutral land of buttered light and warmth, a bowl of stew, good bare brick and wood, homely rag rugs, and not a fat, cushioned chair in sight to make him nervous by its abundance. He understood fire and hard angles, could see the snow pecking at the dark window, and so put down his head and slept, still wild with briars and fleas and the witchy smell of the forest.

Each morning he went out, stiff and silent, prickly as a thistle but determined to earn his keep. He cleared the barn of rats, chased away the neighbor's egg-stealing dog. He did not like chickens or goats, but watched as I gathered eggs or milked and strode before me to the house to open the screen door. He began to make peace with the chintz and china, with tea time and the chatter of my typewriter, with a warm bed and good grooming. At night, he checked the doors and windows, roused up fierce as an old soldier at the sound of a knock or the ring of the telephone. We each began to like the company and sat together in grudging contentment by the fire.

By spring, I loved him. He patrolled the house, pointing out holes where the mice got in. He was not handy, yet disrepair worried him – a banging shutter, faucet drip, the scratching of bats in the attic – and I began to fix neglect, bit by bit. He followed the workmen, grumbling and alert to any impertinence, quick to blaze with temper and tough enough to earn respect. He did not like to be crowded or jostled or touched much in any way, and fights were inevitable. Fighting was strung through his wiry body like a separate nervous system, a powerful but damaged electric grid sparking and spitting, casting off hot flares of ferocity. He bore his wounds with stoicism, accepted no compassion – no society - but mine.

He put on weight, muscle and gloss, became sleek and beautiful in a way wonderful to see. He gave in to innate sensuality, drowsed and stretched in the sun, and ambled with cocky self-assurance through the garden, pleased and relaxed in his body, noticing everything. I loved to touch him, and he reclined against me in amusement at my worship. Playfully, he slapped my hand away, rolled out of reach, dared me to subjugate my pride and chase after him. I did. He knew he was handsome, gleaming like a jet idol, full of himself, cruelly flirtatious, swaggering. The summer was a fat lazy time of love and indulgence; I began to think even he had succumbed to its golden charm.

I barely remembered the time without him. He no longer resembled the starveling vagabond of the past winter, had even mellowed in his violence and suspicion. October brought more than a chill and the scent of bonfires, though, and he spent long hours beside the jack-o-lanterns on the porch, watching the leaves crisp and blush and float to earth, smelling the wild sadness in the air, the dying of the light. It is a traveling time of year. The wind seems to beckon, to suggest a journey to restless feet, to tug at the soul with the promise of finding home, true north, the end of the rainbow. Fly with the leaves, it says. I knew he was listening to that voice, looking out at the forest deeps, at the ashen, gilt-edged shadows full of dim romance. I could only await his decision.

The Boarder

A partnership. It formed in spite of my reluctance and his hard independence. I opened, he softened, and a partnership bloomed. I only accept women boarders; he likes it that way, likes their quiet voices and gentle touches, their generosity and admiration. He curls on their laps and allows them to stroke his plush fur, to tickle his whiskers and compliment him. He enjoys a good book by the fire, a swinging nap in the hammock, a saucer of cream on holidays. He is the man of the house, and takes his nightly patrols seriously, looking after his ladies. His fierceness is reserved for occasional vermin and rude workmen; he has adopted the polished, reserved hospitality of a country squire. He watches visitors with polite disdain, the steel claws flexed and sheathed within the velvet gloves, vigilant against any villainy. And though he haunts the woods and fields, indulging in bloody mayhem among the autumn cornstalks, he returns at dusk to dine and to retire in gentlemanly fashion, purring.

Rumpledsilkskin

Jim and Marion Tupper wanted a house in the country. More than that, they wanted a life in the country – the kind of breezy repose that comprised puttering in a garden (a tidy and mature garden, of course, ready and waiting to be puttered in), lawn games, and family picnics. They envisioned their three children capering after fireflies through blue summer dusk, or building snowmen in the gathering grey wool of a winter's evening, the blazing Christmas tree casting its blinking gold spell from a front window. They dreamed of a house with rustic charm and well-appointed with every modern convenience, these almost mutually exclusive modes of existence never clashing in their innocent fantasies of bucolic bliss. Jim would settle in to write his next book, and Marion would have a garden. Never mind that Marion had never grown anything more challenging than a spider plant. She was sure she had a green thumb beneath her perfect manicure.

On a wet spring day, the Tuppers straggled from the last house on their real estate agent's list, exhausted and disabused of their glowing dream. How could they have known that a life in the country would present so many impediments to their comfort and convenience? The house agent, a dapper little man from the Welcome Home Agency in St. John's Port, was equally exhausted with the Tuppers. Nearly ready to concede defeat, he had called his office one last time to find if any other listings had appeared since they had embarked on their search that morning. To his delight, his secretary informed him that a flyer had come over the fax line just minutes before. She had never heard of the agency, whose name had been mangled by the machine.

"It looks like Food Spell, but it's probably Good Sell," she said, laughing. "Honestly, Paul, you've got to do something about that machine. It nearly chewed off the top of the paper this time."

Good Sell? Paul had never heard of them either, but new competitors were popping up all the time. Whoever they were, they'd chosen a terrible name.

"Never mind about the fax machine, Sara. Shoot me a number and an agent's name so I can get rid of these lookie-loos."

He was surprised at the new agency's location – there was very little business to be done on that side of the river – but he made the call with relief, smiling and nodding at the Tuppers who were standing forlornly by their car. The Good Sell agent sounded enthusiastic. It was probably her first chance at a big commission. She said she would meet the Tuppers at the house and gave Paul excellent directions.

Hanging up, Paul strode up to Jim Tupper and said, "You're in luck! There's a house that sounds perfect for your family just across the river. Beautiful country over there. I've got directions; the agent is expecting you."

"What? We've got to find our way there by ourselves?" Jim was getting testy. This house hunt had been grueling.

Marion put her hand on his arm. "It's alright, Jim. It's the last house today, and it will be a nice peaceful drive in the country for us."

They'd been driving all over the damn country all day. Jim had never seen so much wildlife outside of a zoo. Marion was giving him that earnest look that he knew hid an iron will, and he sighed and took Paul's hastily sketched map.

The tiny village of Wickeford Mills, where they fetched up at last, looked every inch the quaint ghost of colonial history. It was as picturesque and quiet as they could have wished, surrounded as it was by mile after mile of utter wilderness. Its beauty was a fortress. As their car approached the steel truss bridge that spanned the foaming Wicke River, their cell phones ceased communication with the outside world.

The village received them in a brawny huddle of rain slick stone and shaggy hedges. The poker-faced houses puffed lazy curls of smoke onto the leaden sky. The scrutiny of the few locals they saw was frank and ambivalent. Before the Tuppers could form any other impressions of the place, they were away from the houses, bouncing along the wilder half of Rural Route 9 where the tenacious flora pried at the cracked and rubbly macadam, and the woods sprang up to the verge of the road with startling alacrity. At a slight depression in the palisade of the woods, they found the lane they sought. With the trees huddled around and over it, it looked like a dark and forbidding hole. Squaring his shoulders, Jim turned in, passing a narrow open booth with a rough wooden bench inside, its splintery architecture painted a stark white so long ago that it had faded to the color of morning fog.

"That's where the kids will wait for the school bus," he said, pointing at the leaning structure.

Marion's eyes grew wide. "What, in that? It's falling over. Jim, this can't be the right house. The agent said it had a wonderful garden, and all I see is woods."

Just then, they came out of the trees before the dark timbered dazzle of October House. Its Tudor slopes and creamy stucco hide had a rough elegance not at odds with its sylvan surroundings. Its muscular chimneypots promised the pleasures of real wood fires, and its diamond-paned windows of antique glass looked out on the gardens through the bubbles and ripples of another time. The gardens girded the house on three sides, walled away behind an intimidating hedge of ancient box. A tall gated arbor penetrated the hedge, written all over with the calligraphy of a Chinese wisteria, voluptuous in its mid-March nakedness. Marion's mouth formed a little O, and her breath rushed out on a squeak of delight. She danced in her seat, eager to plumb the mysteries of the hidden garden.

The rugged, puddled dirt lane turned into a gravel drive that encircled a venerable clump of birches. Jim orbited these ghostly emissaries of the forest and parked, wondering if the house agent had arrived. He hoped this was it, *the* house, the navel of his family's new life. It was a handsome house from the outside, and looked to be in good repair. If it was a bit isolated, he was sure the serenity and beauty of the woods offset any aspect of loneliness or...eeriness. He got out of the car and rounded it to his wife's door, noting how the *thunk* of the closing car door and the crunch of his feet on the gravel seemed muffled and far away, as sounds in a dream. The woods produced its own atmosphere, and seemed to crouch around them in anticipation. He glanced sidelong into the thick of it, no more than ten feet from him. It did not blend into the clearing and garden of the house, but stopped its march short with all its powerful ranks held in abeyance as though by some charm. Jim thought he could feel the eager press of its force against that of the house; it was as real as the *skreek* of bare branches on glass, and yet no wild tree touched October House or stood within the magic circle of its garden.

The house agent, Kathryn Morse, emerged from the front door and pounced clumsily toward them. Her feet were encased in large, unwieldy black rubber rain boots, comically at odds with her reserved skirt and jacket, and she squelched as she walked. She was armed with a determined toothpaste ad smile.

"Isn't this gorgeous," she said, waving at the house and the breathless woods. "Plenty of space for the kids to run and play, for entertaining in style, and there's that garden I heard you wanted, Mrs. Tupper."

Kathryn's eyes rolled a bit wildly, and she shied like a frightened horse at the sudden explosion of a pair of doves from the woodland boundary. *Boo!* Jim thought, and shivered as a brief shower of icy rain began to fall. They rushed inside the house laughing and gasping, glad to be away from the dour regard of the forest.

The echoing rooms of October House suppressed their mirth. It was not a bright place, nor was it precisely dark. Plenty of cold, clear light penetrated its many windows, but was subdued and digested by the stiff and watchful atmosphere inside. The ceilings flew away and were lost in swaths of gloom among the dark exposed rafters. Shadows hung in the numerous odd nooks and corners like sable sheets of cobweb. Rain scratched and tittered in the massive throats of the chimneys. The house was too solid to creak and groan, so it whispered instead and gnawed on the equinoctial light until all its sharp gleaming edges were reduced to dimness.

Irrepressible, Marion wandered through the rooms chattering and smiling, dragging her drapery swatches and paint chips from her enormous red leather bag, oblivious to the fact that she was being muted. Her high, piping voice came to Jim's ear as a distant murmur. He stood just inside the empty library, feeling wrapped in cotton. Something was strange here. The house was undeniably beautiful and spacious. It appealed to his eye, as tempting as the witch's apple must have seemed to Snow White. He looked about the large quiet room, and the house looked back at him from a thousand shadows.

"Mr. Tupper?" Kathryn Morse's pale face floated into view in the doorway. Her professional, high-wattage smile looked pained, hung on her lips by an act of will. Her ridiculous boots made damp quacking sounds against the wood floors. "The rain has stopped and Mrs. Tupper would like to see the gardens. Would you like to come?"

Jim followed the women across the wide entry hall into the dining room, where French doors let them out onto a slate patio. The rain-sequined garden jostled and strained against the low iron railing, as vivacious and full of fun as the house was reserved. Mossy paths led away in three directions through brawny, mature shrubberies and groves of small ornamental trees, past beds of unknown sleepers that seemed to vibrate with banked energy. Mist rose from the ground and made its sinuous way along the paths, lying smokily over the garden's feet. The little trees were studded with tough red buds and crystals of rain. Cold water dripped from their branches and welled up from the loam. The garden was alive with rustlings and chirps, the soft percussion of birds' wings and the mysterious conversation of water trickling under the ground. Marion and Kathryn gabbled on about bulbs and woody propagation, Marion consulting a gardening book produced from her prodigious red bag, and Jim fell behind, alone with his thoughts. Turning to look back at the house, he was surprised to see only its steep roofs rising from the profusion of plantings, the tiny dormer windows of the attic blinking in the grey light like sharp black eyes.

They tramped about until they came to the crumbling wall at the property's edge. A small stone potting shed, half buried in honeysuckle vines, stood sentry at a leaning gate. Beyond the Gothic gate posts, its roots against a narrow verge of wiry grass in a line as sharp as one drawn with a ruler, the Johns Woods loomed in a dark tangle. The three of them stood at the gate, looking out in silence.

Finally, Kathryn cleared her throat and said, "Those woods stretch for miles. They're dense and easy to get lost in. I'd caution the children –"

"What's that?" Marion interrupted, pointing to a small bare spot just under the black eaves of the forest. It was a circle of toadstools and spongy moss spangled with violets and dogtooth lilies, quite distinct from the surrounding root scrabble and leaf stratum. The center of the ring was a carpet of short thick grass, bare of woodsy detritus as though vacuumed, where not a single flower grew.

Kathryn blushed. "Well, it's a fairy ring. That's what some call it. You come across them in the woods from time to time." She turned her protuberant, lichen-colored eyes on the Tuppers, and dropped her voice to a hoarse passionate whisper. "Don't step inside it. Never, never, never!"

In the next instant, her smile and her perky voice were restored. "Well, what do you think? Shall we go and do some paperwork?"

If Marion had been startled by the agent's strange lapse, she forgot it now. "Oh yes! Jim? Please, this is the one. The kids will love it!"

They made their way back to the house and congregated, dripping, in the kitchen. Kathryn pulled a roll of thick, yellowed papers from her briefcase, and smoothed open the quaint scroll on the long plank table. Jim, with a glance around at the colonial era kitchen, wondered if she would next produce a quill pen. But Kathryn flourished a perfectly mundane ball point, and the Tuppers signed the papers.

The children did not love October House. They huddled together in the enormous entry hall, clustered in front of a fireplace that could have held all three of them. Ten-year-old Charles, as the eldest, spoke for the trio and voiced his reservations immediately.

"It's old and dark. It's creepy." He looked up at the tenebrous vault of the ceiling, then into the maw of the fireplace. He pointed at the heavy stone structure. "That thing looks like it wants to eat us."

Seven-year-old Adam and five-year-old Amelia Rose, wearing the woeful expressions of orphans newly arrived at the workhouse, shuffled further from the hearth.

Marion was exasperated. "For Heaven's sake, Charles, the things you say. The house is just empty and needs a little redecoration. Then it will look bright and cheerful. Why don't you kids run upstairs and pick out your bedrooms?"

Thank goodness Ms. Morse, who had stopped by to welcome them and to offer Good Sell's complimentary moving services, had gone before hearing Charles's bleak opinion of the house. She looked at Jim. He was always able to jolly the children along when they were feeling temperamental. He gave Charles a grin and ruffled the boy's hair, which made Marion frown.

"I'll take a look at this old monster," he said, kicking at the stone fireplace. "Better have the chimneys cleaned before we have any fires."

He turned to Marion. "I thought I'd zip down to the city if you don't need me. Have lunch with old Clyde and talk over some things."

Clyde was Jim's agent, a man Marion was certain was an alcoholic. She pinched her lips together, but then laughed. It would be better not to have Jim under foot as she hashed out plans with her decorator. She'd call Andrew first thing after her husband left.

"Fine. Abandon me. I have plenty to keep me busy."

Jim kissed the top of her head, and moved to squat in front of the fireplace, craning his neck to look up the black throat of the chimney. "I'll poke around in here first. I'll stop on my way home and pick up dinner, shall I? Chinese?"

Marion's eyes were already turned to the dining room walls, where she thought a royal blue paper in a chinoiserie pattern of birds would be handsome above the walnut paneled wainscoting. She barely heard Jim as she pulled out her swatch book, meaning to search for the precise paper she had in mind. Nor did she pay any heed when the children ventured through the room and slipped out the French doors into the garden.

Once among the vigorous denizens of the garden, the oppressive miasma of October House lifted from the children. Here were tunnels and forts of shrubbery, stone benches presided over by stone angels, serpentine paths of velvet moss and the thread-slender secret paths of animals that wound through the thickets. There were subtle descending levels that caused the house to recede as though the garden stretched a mile. There was a koi pond, empty now of fish, its winter netting dragging in brackish rainwater, its stones slippery. Best of all, at the bottom of the garden, there was a little house and a newly constructed gate that hung like an exhausted tongue from the ancient crooked gateposts.

Adam rushed toward the petite stone house. "Hey, you guys, this must be the *potting shed.*"

He spoke the words with reverence. The potting shed, it had been explained to them, was strictly off limits. Their father had pronounced it unsafe. Likewise, the gate that led into the forest was never to be opened. The children stared through the gate. The Johns Woods were dark and still, unlit by the pale sunlight. They were not inviting; in fact, they were frightening.

The children turned their attention to the wonderful potting shed. The kneeling building fascinated them, but there seemed no hope of entering it. The plank door was forever shut, the weight of the crumbling slate roof having driven it into the soft earth. The boys roamed about it, pushing through the tall stands of shriveled hollyhock and weeds that grew tight against the cold stone.

Charles saw the tiny window first, high up and slightly ajar. "Look! I'll lift Amelia Rose up, and she can crawl through the window." He gave his sister a stern look. "Amelia, you'll have to tell us what's in there, so don't be scared, ok?"

Tiny Amelia Rose put her hands on her hips and thrust out her chest. "I'm not scared!"

"Good. You're our scout. So tell us everything you see." Charles dropped to his hands and knees on the damp grass. "Climb up on my shoulders."

Adam studied the window with a frown. "What if she gets stuck? We won't be able to pull her out. What if Mom comes looking for us?"

Charles snorted in disgust. "Mom's busy with her wallpaper. She's not going to come down here." He struggled to his feet with Amelia Rose riding on his shoulders, clutching his hair. "Come on, if we're going to look."

Charles grasped her hands as Amelia Rose stood shakily on his shoulders, her sodden sneakers slipping until he seized her by the calves. She was high enough to see in the little window, but the glass was grimed with dirt and cobwebs. She pried at the window frame, raining paint splinters on the two boys, and the window opened in a series of groaning jerks. She thrust her head through, but the interior of the potting shed was a murky study in charcoal.

"Hurry up," hissed Charles. "You're heavy."

Without a word, Amelia Rose wriggled through the window and dropped through dark air on the other side. She landed with an abrupt thump on a bare potting bench, and peered into the dusty gloom. Broken terra cotta pots, rusty trowels and rakes, and mouse-eaten gloves littered the floor. Rolled bales of rabbit fence sagged in a corner. Vines had thrust their strong fingers through the roof and walls, beginning the slow work of pulling apart the stones and timbers. Amelia Rose crouched on the potting bench and breathed lightly, listening. At first, it seemed as though the potting shed were holding its breath, watching her the way October House had watched her when she entered it. A whisper of cold brushed her cheek, and she jerked to her feet, ready to shimmy back out the window. But then, she heard a faint scuffling from beneath the potting bench, a tiny cry. Kneeling, she peeked over the edge. A fury of fur and tangled bird netting erupted from the darkness, spitting and wrestling. Amelia Rose screamed and scuttled backward.

"What is it? 'Melia! What's going on?" Charles and Adam scrabbled in alarm at the stone wall outside.

Amelia Rose's grimy face appeared at the window. "There's a kitty in here, all tangled in a net. I'm going to get it and hand it out. Wait."

When Amelia Rose and the cat were safe in the garden, the children examined their new pet. It was a small thin creature with smoky fur that stuck up in tufts and snarls. Its tail was hung with twigs and nettles. It sported the bandit mask and dark stockings of a Siamese, and its eyes were clear, cold blue. It lay, purring and preening its scruffiness, in Amelia Rose's lap.

Adam stroked its head. "What should we name it?"

"How about Ugly?"

"That's mean Charles!" Amelia Rose and the cat glared in tandem.

Charles reached for the cat's tail and tugged it aside. "Well, it's a girl. I guess it should have a girlie name."

The cat, growling, switched her tail from Charles's fingers and laid her ears against her skull.

"I want to name her Rumpledsilkskin." Amelia Rose soothed the cat back to rumbling complacency. "Mommy read that to me yesterday."

Charles rolled his eyes. "It's *Rumplestiltskin*, dummy."

Adam laughed. "I like 'Melia's name better. The cat is all rumpled up, and she's silky, too. I think she's hungry."

The cavernous kitchen of October House had been well stocked, pantry and refrigerator, with everything a hungry young family might need in the midst of a household move. The house agent lady had made sure of it. She had said it was part of her "comprehensive service", Charles remembered, and had shown her sharp little teeth. She had gone on to assure them that she would engage the movers and that she would send another lady from the village to be their housekeeper. They had never had a housekeeper before. Charles was unsure what such a person did, but Mom had seemed pretty happy about it.

Now, as he led his siblings along the narrow maintenance walkway that wound between the azalea beds and the side of the house, Charles hoped the housekeeper hadn't shown up yet. He peeked in each window as they crept past, Amelia Rose tiptoeing behind him and Adam following with Rumpledsilkskin tucked inside his jacket. He saw their mother in what the agent lady had called the "morning room". She stretched in elegant repose along the bloated expanse of a sofa left by the previous owner.

Charles knew that the sofa was hard and musty-smelling because he had bounced on it before Mom gave that breathy little shriek she used when she caught one of them doing something bad. *That is a priceless antique, Charles!* she had scolded. *You are not to sit on it!* The last bit she had addressed to all three of them. It was the agent lady who had told him that the thing was stuffed with horsehair, and he had recoiled from it in disgust, envisioning several entire horses encased in the pythonesque gut of the sofa, their knobby bones and upturned hooves creating the lumpy terrain under the red velvet. Mom was talking on the cordless phone, probably to Dad back in the city, or maybe to the decorator guy who gave her the swatch books. The books were open on the floor by the sofa with their streamers of fabric and wallpaper askew.

"Come on," Charles whispered, pulling on Amelia Rose's sleeve. "Be quiet. We can get in through the pantry door."

The children rounded the house and slipped in the through the low oaken door. The pantry was little more than a short hallway, lined on one side with age-blackened wooden shelves that went right up to the ceiling. The topmost shelves were lost in darkness that the high stained-glass windows opposite them did little to illuminate. Beneath the windows was a stark granite counter and two immense farm sinks, also granite, exuding a wintry cold into the narrow space.

"Wait a minute," Charles breathed. "That housekeeper lady might be in there."

He peered around the corner into the kitchen, and saw nothing but the black broad-hipped stove from another century, the bare faintly chiming pot hooks that dangled high above, the long plain plank table, and the squat arch of the brick fireplace with its crooked hearth that gave it the mumbling expression of a toothless mouth.

"OK, let's go."

The children scurried about the room, barely suppressing their laughter as they organized a feast for Rumpledsilkskin. The cat sat on the long farmhouse table, and watched with interest as first tuna, then milk, and then shredded cheddar appeared in saucers before her. She ate some of everything, seeming to expand in front of their eyes, and then leaped to the floor and settled on the hearth to wash her face and ears. Amelia Rose, who had a great respect for personal grooming when she wasn't adventuring with her brothers, pulled a small hairbrush from her jacket pocket and began to stroke the lean slope of the cat's back, following the long sooty line of her tail to its tip. Rumpledsilkskin's fur began to gleam like fog in the moonlight.

"She's so beautiful. Do you think Mom will let us keep her?" Amelia Rose's face was wistful.

"Probably not," said Adam. "She wouldn't let us get a dog. I don't think she'll want a cat, either." He looked up at Charles, who was clearing away the dirty saucers. "We'll have to hide her, that's all."

Charles snorted. "Oh, that'll be easy."

But sarcasm was lost on Adam and Amelia Rose, who waited to hear the solution to their problem. The slamming of the heavy pantry door interrupted their strategizing and brought them to frightened attention. With their eyes trained on the doorway to the pantry, none of them saw Rumpledsilkskin stand, stretch, and with a swish of her tail, vanish up the chimney.

A woman entered the kitchen, her arms laden with brown paper grocery bags, a basket with a blue and white checked cloth over it, and a net bag full of oranges. Her eyes were hidden under the wide brim of a soft hat like the gardening hat their mother had bought on the drive here. Unruly curls peeked out here and there, pale blonde or maybe white. She was short and square, with a mounded bosom like a cartoon hen, and her skinny ankles stuck out from under the hem of her long grey skirt, clad in severe black stockings. Her feet were solid and shapeless as bricks in large boiled wool clogs. The children goggled at her as she stumped up to the table and unburdened herself with a gusty sigh. She raked the hat from her head, sailed it onto a peg beside the pantry doorway, and fixed them with a pair of frosty pale green eyes that held no surprise at their presence.

"Well, young Tuppers. I'm Nora, your new housekeeper." Nora scrutinized them, bending down to chuck Amelia Rose under the chin. "Now aren't you a pretty one?" The pale fingers moved to test the silk of Amelia Rose's chestnut ringlets. "Yes, a very pretty one."

The housekeeper straightened and fixed her strange eyes on Adam and Charles. "Boys. Full of nastiness the both of you, no doubt. Sturdy chaps, though." She smiled toothily, and placed a hand on each of their shoulders and kneaded. "I'm sure we'll be the best of friends. Now, scoot off and let your mother know I've come…unless there's something you want in the kitchen?" Nora shot a sly, sidelong glance at the hearth. "Cat got your tongues? Shoo, then!"

She flapped the voluminous apron that overlay her skirt, and the children scattered like chickens.

Marion Tupper paced the length of the morning room, and then dropped to her knees. She scribbled with furious speed on a little notepad, using the wide window ledge for a desk. Fourteen feet. She calculated the desired ratio of Aubusson carpet to length of room, noting that pastels would be preferable to jewel tones. From her crouch by the window, she observed with a jaded eye the fat horsehair sofa across the room. Red velvet would never do. She would have it stripped and reupholstered, perhaps in pale yellow and grey stripes, and re-stuffed with something less grotesque and more comfortable. She wanted to love the sofa. It was valuable and presented a classic silhouette she thought sophisticated. Its scalloped back and curved legs could be feminine and grace-ful, although the claw feet spoiled the effect. Yes, she wanted to love it, but it rebuffed her. It was a vast brooding monster of a piece, and just looking at it disfigured her delicate vision of what the morning room could become. She sighed and massaged her temples. She was going to have a headache.

From the hallway came the sound of stampeding sneakered feet. Marion stood, a vertical line of annoyance creasing her brow. The children knew bet-ter than to gallop through the house like wild things. She moved to the door, intending to scold them, but she was overwhelmed as they swarmed around her, all talking at once.

Marion clapped her hands twice in sharp, school-marm fashion. "Hush! Where have you children been? I wanted to discuss your bedrooms with you." Before the babble could erupt again, she went on. "Never mind that now. Has Mrs. Erlman arrived?"

"If you mean the housekeeper, she's in the kitchen. She says her name's Nora, and she's awful." Charles crossed his arms on his chest and gave Marion a look that was both hurt and disapproving. She thought he looked remarkably like his father just then, and that made her peevish.

"That will be enough cheek from you, young man. All of you, go upstairs and wash up for lunch. You look like a band of chimney sweeps."

She watched them drag up the shadowy staircase wearing gloomy faces before she set off for the kitchen. Really, it was almost too much to watch over all three while trying to organize the redecorating. She spared a petulant, dag-gered thought for Jim who was probably preparing to have lunch with his agent at the Orient Tea Room. And here was a strange thing! A shoe, one of Jim's ratty sneakers, lay on its side on the enormous hearth in front of the entry hall fireplace. She bent to pick it up and saw a scrap of cloth in the firebox. Closer inspection showed it to be a ripped patch of the tee shirt Jim had worn that morning. Imagine! The man was reverting to the careless slob of his student days. To leave his shoe just lying there! Still, she hesitated to touch the bit of cloth lying on the andirons. A thin sift of soot rustled down the chimney. She peeked upward, but it was black as a hat and she could see nothing. The small-voiced drum in her temples began to beat with a little more vigor. Still carrying the shoe, she went to meet Mrs. Erlman.

The kitchen had shrugged off the aspect of menacing vacancy that Marion had at first found so forbidding. Now it seemed a warm and bustling place with a low fire burning and casting a cheery glow on the copper pots suspended from the pot hooks. A round-bellied cast iron pot bubbled and chortled on the range top, puffing a savory steam onto the air. There was an enormous batter bowl full of fruit on the table, and the table itself wore a long woven runner of bright cranberry. Bundles of dried herbs tied with pretty ribbon hung in the windows.

"Oh! How wonderful," Marion exclaimed. It was as though a page from one of her decorating magazines had come to life.

A pale, curly head popped out of the pantry. Merry green eyes twinkled, wreathed in laugh lines. "Why, thank you, Mrs. Tupper. I've just been getting things ready for lunch." The curly head emerged on a short, matronly body in stout shoes. "I'm Nora Erlman, and very pleased to meet you."

Marion found herself smiling for the first time that day. "I'm so glad you've come, Mrs. Erlman. I've been on the phone with my decorator all morning, trying to make him understand what I want, and I'm exhausted. I don't know how I would have managed lunch for the children." She waved a hand at the kitchen. "You've worked magic in here."

"Please, call me Nora. Why don't you sit down and I'll brew you up a cup of tea. You look all in, if you don't mind my saying."

Nora hung a kettle on a hook and swung it into the fireplace. Marion, who appreciated the look of the old kitchen if not its application, was charmed. She watched as Nora chose a few of the bundled herbs in the window and snipped some sprigs from each with a tiny scissors she drew from her apron pocket. From another apron pocket, Nora withdrew a copper tea ball in the shape of an acorn, into which she crumbled the herbs. The kettle was rumbling in the fireplace. Nora took a heavy earthenware mug down from the mantle, plunked the tea ball in it, and filled it with the hot water.

"Here you are. This will fix what ails you."

Marion looked down into the dark green liquid and inhaled the aromatic steam. She tasted. Something sweet and woodsy and warm curled over her tongue, and then through her limbs. The drumming in her temples ceased, and her body grew heavy with contentment. Half dreaming, she drank it all.

"Mmm. It's so good, Nora. What herbs are these?" Marion's eyes drooped, but her sense of well-being was complete.

Nora smiled. "Oh, a pinch of this, a smidgen of that. You look very tired Mrs. Tupper. Why don't you go have a little nap on the sofa in the morning room? I'll see that the children are looked after."

"Yes, thank you. I think I will." The thought of a nap was heavenly. It was so good to be able to relinquish her responsibilities, even for a short time.

Marion rose on legs of cloud and made her way to the morning room. She sank onto the sofa, which felt much softer and deeper than before. Beneath her, the red velvet seemed to shift and undulate. It felt accommodating and warm to her touch, and she nestled deeper, patting the fat cushions. *Gotta reupholster you,* she thought. It was really a very nice sofa. She'd make it beautiful again.

She was so heavy with sleepiness that she was unable to muster more than vague alarm when she heard its clawed feet clicking on the floorboards. It panted and growled softly, like a dog with a bone, and Marion sank further into its embrace. She knew it wasn't a dream; she could feel the sofa stretching and flexing, enveloping her in musty gulps. Panic sent up a single white-hot flare in her brain. She struggled once, feebly, and then she fell into its dark red warmth.

Rumpledsilkskin stalked along the steep roof, lashing her tail in anger. She had been ensnared for too long in the potting shed and things had come undone. She crouched and looked out over the gardens and into the forest. The trees were restless, leaning against the invisible boundary that encircled October House. She knew each one of them, carried a map of their vanguard in her brain, and she could see where a gap had opened. A gnarled hawthorn, an insignificant understory weed, was missing. Rumpledsilkskin sniffed. The smoke and metal burr of sorcery wafted on the cold air. It came from the defiant gap in the forest, and it arose from the house beneath her.

The cat resumed her pacing. She had been lucky to escape the kitchen chimney where she had lingered a while in hopes of eavesdropping, but the Nora-creature had kindled fire. It had tried to make the chimney eat her, but the sleepy old kitchen bricks had only grumbled and fallen back into their age-long doze. Now Rumpledsilkskin approached the next chimney. This one would open into the entry hall fireplace, and it was mammoth. She scrambled up to its wide lip and looked down. A dark vine of some sort had crawled down the throat of the chimney and been roasted; its furred back was soot-blackened and brawny. As she watched, it twitched and shuddered. Something that looked like a skeletal hand dangled from it and scraped against the bricks. That was bad. This chimney was neither sleepy nor friendly.

Another gigantic brick structure stood farther out along an ell of the house. At this one, Rumpledsilkskin detected the scent of the Tupper children. Without further caution, she popped down the chimney and emerged in a bed chamber furnished only with an iron bedstead and a grey, sagging mattress.

The children sat in a row on the edge of the bed, their pale young faces pinched and dejected. October House felt all wrong to them; it made whispers and grumbles and watched their every move. The housekeeper had frightened them with her cold eyes and pinching fingers. They wanted nothing more than to go back to the city where the woods were tame and confined to the park, and the buildings didn't crouch over them like hungry dragons.

Amelia Rose was the first to see the cat slink from the fireplace. "Look, it's Rumpledsilkskin! She's safe!"

The girl slid from the bed and ran to kneel beside the cat, stroking away the ashes and cobwebs that clung to her fur.

MIAOWWW! said Rumpledsilkskin in a mighty voice. She shook her head and tried again, producing a long yowl that ended in a cough. She opened and closed her jaw a few times and said, *RRREKKK!*

"What's the matter with her?" Charles's eyes were round with alarm.

Adam peered at the cat who paced and lashed her tail, stretching her jaw first one way then another.

"I think she's trying to talk."

"Cats can't talk!"

Rumpledsilkskin sprang upon the bed and tore at the mattress in fury. She fixed the hot blue sparks of her eyes on Charles and said, "YRRESSS! Talk."

The word was unmistakable, even if delivered in a voice that was a cross between a rusty hinge and the rasp of sandpaper on rough wood. Adam and Charles gaped at the cat, and Amelia Rose laughed and clapped her hands in glee.

Rumpledsilkskin sat and curled her tail around her paws, pleased to have their undivided attention. With a purring roll of the R, she said, "Rrrun!"

She sneezed and said, "Norrra bad. Rrrun!"

The children fell back in a knot and discussed what they had heard, casting glances over their shoulders at Rumpledsilkskin, now calmly grooming her fur. Talking cats were not excluded from their lists of possibilities, and though Charles struggled a bit with this astonishing development, Adam and Amelia Rose accepted it with very little incredulity. The magic of make-believe still informed their days; their nights were glowing palaces of dream. And if they had never feared the dark, still they were not unaware that nightmares sometimes walked the palace halls — or that they even lurked in the more shadowy day places. Hadn't their parents warned them never to talk to strangers? And what was Nora but the very definition of a stranger? The logic was unimpeachable, and Rumpledsilkskin's warning fell on fertile ground.

They could make no use of the cat's advice to run away. Where could they go? They would have to find a way to oust Nora. Maybe their parents would see that this move had been a mistake. Charles approached the cat, steady and resolved as a knight before battle.

"What should we do?"

It was noon, the fulcrum of the day. The Tupper children filed in silence along the upstairs hallway, and then down the long-throated half spiral of the staircase, like tightrope walkers. They were balanced on the fast-eroding point of midday, and Rumpledsilkskin stalked behind them urging them to hurry. From the tall windows they could see the massing of a storm. Bales of bruised cloud sailed into the tops of the trees, and where the mist rose from the forest floor, the Johns Woods was wedded to the angry sky. The day would slide quickly into the mouth of night, and they had much to do before then.

At the foot of the staircase, they stopped to peer down the entry hall toward the kitchen. The sound of tuneless humming, a contented, mindless sound, came to them. Charles, on his hands and knees, leaned around the newel post.

"I see Nora," he whispered. "She's in the morning room; I just saw her go past the doorway." He drew back onto the bottom stair, where Adam and Amelia Rose huddled against the wall. "At least, I think it was her. It looked sort of tallish, and Nora's short and fat."

Rumpledsilkskin, sitting on Adam's lap, hissed and fluffed her tail. "Norrra change," she said in her rust and rasp voice. "Not woman. Not belong here."

Charles felt his scalp creep. He felt hot and cold at once, like he might be feverish. He looked at Adam, whose face seemed to be all eyes, and at Amelia Rose's white, pinched nostrils. They were scared almost to death, and he wasn't much better off.

"Where's Mommy? She can help us." Amelia Rose turned a beseeching gaze on Rumpledsilkskin.

The cat stared back, and the fierce blue glare of her eyes softened. Placing a paw on Amelia Rose's arm, she purred, "Gone. Man and woman, both gone. House eat."

Adam made a strangled little hiccough, and dashed sudden tears from his eyes, but Amelia Rose only grew grim and stony. Charles felt his stomach fall. If it were true, they were orphaned, alone in a world where monsters walked - and he knew the monster that had orchestrated it all. Pushing down his fear and grief, he wiped his sweaty palms against his knees and stood.

"OK, we all know the plan. Is everyone ready?"

Three pairs of eyes met his, three heads nodded. Without a weapon but his wits, with no confederates but a talking cat and the younger siblings he had always dominated and looked after, Charles prepared to face the wood witch.

That was what Rumpledsilkskin had called her. When they had overcome their astonishment at the cat's verbal skill, they had sat in a ring on the cold parquet floor of the bedroom and listened as Rumpledsilkskin explained their danger. October House had never really been for sale. It had sat empty for long years, brooding over its little domain of garden and settling by increments into the earth, and no one came to save it. Could they not see its decrepitude? And the house agent lady, with her huge black boots and her eyes like icy jade – did she remind them of anyone? All was glamour, trickery, and the thing they knew as Nora had created it. Rumpledsilkskin growled and urged them to see with more than their eyes. She urged them to see with their souls.

"If she's not a person, what is she," Adam asked.

Rumpledsilkskin's eyes squinched down into two simmering slits of blue fire.

"Wood witch. Bad."

The cat seemed to consider something, then added, "Small, though. Can catch her."

She lifted a dark fist, the steely claws sheathed in the velvet glove, and gave it a lick.

Charles leaned forward. "What do you mean, you can catch her?"

"Not I. We." The inscrutable sharp-wedge face swung toward him. "Make trap. Need bait."

He didn't like the sound of that. "What kind of trap?"

"Rrring. Ring to catch, ring to hold."

A ring? He thought of his mother's wedding ring, the one with all the diamonds and the green stones called emeralds. She was always complaining about how it swung around on her finger. She said it needed to be *sized*, whatever that was, and would invariably go on to talk about her diet and the fifteen pounds she'd lost. Did the cat mean a ring like that?

"You mean like a wedding ring?"

The cat seemed impatient now, switching her tail across the dusty floor, her ears lowered. She glanced out the windows to where the sky above the woods was turning an ugly grey-blue.

"Watch," she hissed.

She stood and turned about three times as though she were making a bed for herself. Charles had seen his cousin's cat do the same thing every time it wanted to nestle somewhere for a nap, although it had accomplished it with a lot of kneading and rumbling. But he had never seen anything like the pale ring of blue foxfire that rose flickering around Rumpledsilkskin.

Adam and Amelia Rose gasped. The cat tiptoed from the center of the glow, and it ghosted and shivered on the dark mahogany.

"Rrring," said the cat, with a hint of pride in her voice. She swatted at the eerie light, and it vanished like sun-kissed fog.

His hand on the newel post, Charles took a deep breath and looked over his shoulder at the others. They were on their feet, pale but determined. As one, they crept down the hall to the dining room doorway. Amelia Rose and Rumpledsilkskin scampered across the room and Amelia eased open the French door, just enough for the two for them to slip through, and then closed it with a tiny rattle. The girl looked back once, and then she and the cat vanished down the path that led to the kitchen herb garden.

The monotonous humming coming from the morning room stopped. A tall slender shadow crossed the threshold, and Nora's voice called out, "Children? Are you out there?"

Quick as a snake, the pale curly head darted from the doorway, the little green eyes shining silver in the gathering stormlight. Charles and Adam were already moving toward her, and the severe line of her mouth softened into a smile that Charles thought was as fake as last year's Christmas tree.

"We were hungry. Is lunch ready?" He pressed into the morning room. He hated to brush so near the witch, but he wanted to see if Mom was in there. "How come you're in here?"

Nora fell back, surprised. She moved to the casement windows and fussed with the locks. "There's a storm a-brewing. I was checking the windows."

Charles looked around, but there was nothing in the room but the hateful red sofa. It bulged more than ever, its frayed underbelly hanging between its clawed feet like a fat man's paunch. He glared at it, hoping every spring was sprung and that it would soon find itself at a landfill, and he saw something in the shadow of its heft. Something small that glimmered white and emerald in the darkening light. His mother's wedding ring!

A calm fury descended on him, and he turned to Nora who still fussed at the windows. "Where's Mom," he asked.

The wood witch turned a wide, white smile on him that did not reach her eyes. "Why, she had a few errands to run. She left me to see to you, so why don't we go to the kitchen and have a bite." She snapped her teeth on the last word, and reached a hand toward his shoulder.

"I'm starved," Adam yelled from the doorway.

The words punctured the doomy atmosphere like the magic dart of a counter spell, and Charles slipped away from Nora to join his brother. With the wood witch behind them, the boys marched to the kitchen.

The garden looked dead in the leaden light of the coming storm. All the upward thrusting green energy of the morning was stilled, and the cold had crept in from the huddled forest, sliding along the pathways like air released from a crypt. Amelia Rose followed Rumpledsilkskin into the herb beds where last year's stalks and pods talked among themselves in worried whispers. The cat wove through the deep mulched beds, between thick grey mats of mint and thyme like snarls of hair, around the stiff canes of roses that wore wicked thorns gleaming in the gloom like iron barbs, through the dense scribble of oregano, to the edge of the garden where she found the plant she sought.

"Yarrow," rasped Rumpledsilkskin in what, for her, passed for a whisper. "Binding. Strong."

The yarrow looked limp and sad to Amelia Rose. Nests of fine ferny foliage sprawled on the ground, but it was sparse and battered. Dry stalks poked up from it and came away in her hand when she tugged, trailing dark clots of earth and palsied roots. She had stepped on some of it, and an astringent smell that caused the inside of her mouth to pucker rose from the bed. At least the scent was strong.

"It's all dead, Rumpledsilkskin. The winter killed it, and it isn't alive again yet."

Dismay welled up, and she hitched a tiny sob. She was cold and scared. Her brothers were in the house with the bad witch. Her mommy and daddy were gone, and Rumpledsilkskin said the house had *eaten* them! She feared it was too late for any of them to be saved, and a tear slipped over her round pink cheek.

The cat growled and began kneading the yarrow. "No. Strong. Not dead. Make rrring."

With all four paws, she raked and tugged at the lank foliage, dragging it into a rough circular shape. Amelia Rose glanced at the house, and then fell to her knees beside the cat and began to weave the cold pungent yarrow into a shaggy kind of wreath. The circlet was more than three feet across, encompassing the whole patch. The fragrance of the bruised yarrow was intense, a sharp green knife that sliced the muzzy grey from the air and cleared Amelia Rose's mind of everything but her task. She began to believe that the plant *was* strong, and that it would be fierce enough to snare a nightmare.

When they had completed the wreath, Rumpledsilkskin scratched some of the old leaf litter over it, hiding the shape a bit. The cat scrutinized their handiwork, and then went to the center of the circle and began to turn, turn, turn. The low blue-green flicker of foxfire kindled in the air just above the yarrow wreath, the trap. As the cat spun faster, it ignited with a sigh and raced around the circle, dancing like heat shimmer before sinking into the woven herbs. There it pulsed and glimmered, nearly invisible to the eye, hidden among the leaves and twigs.

Rumpledsilkskin bounded to Amelia Rose's side, her glacial blue eyes sparkling. "Rrring! Now, catch her. Catch wood witch."

Amelia Rose nodded. She didn't think she was afraid anymore, or maybe she was just so scared she couldn't feel it. Whichever was the case, it was time to put their plan into action. She walked to the far side of the ring and reached for one of the razor-barbed rose canes.

Charles and Adam entered the kitchen with their hearts knocking loudly against their ribs. The room was dark except for the dragon red glare of the low fire. Something squatted on the table, and Adam saw that it was a damp chunk of wood, like the thick shoulder of a tree bough, slick and warty with toadstools, and crawling with wood lice and centipedes. He tugged at Charles's sleeve and his brother, alert to every shift of the creeping shadows, mouthed *I see it.*

Charles saw something under the table, too. It was a shoe, one of Dad's, and it looked *gnawed* on. He swallowed the lump that formed in his throat and pasted on a smile as he turned to Nora.

"Mmmm. Something smells good. We're really hungry."

His voice cracked a little on the last word, and Adam thought his brother looked stricken and not happy or hungry at all, but Nora seemed to relax. She waved toward the horrible centerpiece on the table.

"Why don't you boys have some fruit? I'll dish up the soup, and you can eat it in the breakfast nook."

She moved toward the stove where something that smelled like mould and sulphur bubbled and burped in a battered pot, her feet in their unwieldy clogs slapping the stone floor in a peculiar flat-footed way.

"Fruit? I'm not eating any of that," Adam whispered at Charles, recoiling from the table.

Charles grabbed Adam by the hand and dragged him toward the little nook by the window. It was dark in there. The window was curtained by bundles of long dangling roots; their black snaky fingers tapped against the panes. A woody vine grew along the wall and hung from the archway, grasping the wood with stubby white talons studded with tumorous nodules. He thrust Adam into a chair and sat across from him.

"Don't eat anything she gives you, but pretend, ok?" He parted the roots and tried to peer out the window. "I don't see Amelia Rose, but we have to be ready."

Nora loomed up beside them, causing Adam to squeak in terror. She studied them for a few interminable seconds, and then set two malodorous bowls of swampy stew before them. Two rusty spoons clattered to the table after them.

"Eat up, boys. It will make you big and strong."

This seemed to amuse her, and she guffawed and chuckled as she stumped back to the fire where she dropped like a stone into the hickory rocker. A dented copper tub, gone green with verdigris, sat steaming on the hearth. Nora kicked off her wool clogs and submerged her feet with a sigh.

Charles leaned across the table. "Did you see her feet?"

Adam, who had been staring dismally into his soup bowl, looked up and shook his head.

"They're *black*! I thought it was her stockings, but it isn't. And her feet are all knobby and long, like —"

He looked around for a comparison, and his eyes fell on the bundled roots hanging in the window. "Like these roots! She's got feet like tree roots."

The boys stared at each other, horror written on their faces. Adam tried to swallow and found he had no spit. That was when Amelia Rose began to shriek.

CRASH! The copper tub went over, reverberating with a hollow gonging sound, and sending a tidal wave of warm peaty water across the flagstones. Nora leaped to her knobby black feet and sped to the pantry door, duck walking in big lolloping strides. Her skirt, rucked up above her knees, showed scrawny gnarled calves that flexed and creaked like tree limbs in a gale. She threw open the door and thrashed across the stones of the little patio, craning her elongating neck to the left and then to the right.

In the doorway, Adam and Charles watched as squat, dumpy Nora grew taller. Her sharp grey elbows poked through the knit of her cardigan, and her spindly, big-knuckled fingers stretched out like shadows on a wall. Lightning cracked the deep purple sky like an eggshell, and Nora's fine white hair stood out in a sparking eldritch halo.

Amelia Rose continued to howl. The wood witch, unconcerned that her costume was slipping, put her nose in the air and sniffed like a hound. She took three ground-eating strides and vanished around a towering clump of feather reed grasses. She was so fast! Charles hadn't anticipated her frightful speed, and he darted after her, his shoes sliding in the pea gravel that defined the kitchen garden pathways. So intent on catching up was he that he nearly ran into her as he charged around the swaying tufted grass. Adam slid to a stop beside him and sat down hard, almost at the witch's feet.

Amelia Rose sat on the ground in the middle of the herb beds, blubbering and clutching her hand to her chest. The hand was red and dripping, and blood had smeared the front of her jacket and fallen in fat drops on the mulch where she had dropped the thorny rose cane. Her hand really did hurt, and Amelia Rose pulled in a great gulp of air and let out another wail as thunder boomed in the distance.

The wood witch stood as though turned to stone. Only her nose moved, twitching and wrinkling, savoring the rich vermilion smell of the girl's blood. How long had it been since that delicious fragrance had been so close? Her life was a long slow one, and she could not recall. A silver thread of spittle descended from her lip.

She composed her voice and said, "Child, you've hurt yourself. Come here to Nora and let me fix it."

The stupid girl only blinked owlishly, her face red and blotchy from screaming. A fresh, hot bead of blood blossomed on a tiny fingertip and seemed to hold the red world reflected on its curvature. The witch uttered a grating rumble, and the first heavy splatters of rain began to fall in fat liquid detonations. She took a step closer to Amelia Rose, the little pretty one, and then another. Why did the girl not move?

As she took a third step, she saw the ghost of a flicker before she set her foot down, as though the lightning had somehow gotten under the leaves. A trick! With a furious hiss, the wood witch twisted in mid-step to avoid the ring she now saw burning on a sloppy, braided loop of yarrow like a rabbit snare. Did they think they could fool her so easily? She would eat all three of the little brats for this. She would lay them in the forest loam for tenderizing, and then crack their bones for the sweet marrow.

Charles shouted in fear and anger. After all their planning, she was going to get away! He threw himself at her knees as Adam lunged for her ankle. Thunder bellowed around them, Amelia Rose screamed, and another brilliant seam opened in the clouds. The rain swept down in a gust, and the wood witch staggered and screeched as she tried to shake them off. Adam lost his grip and went rolling to the edge of the foxfire ring where he lay stunned for a moment. The witch lifted her foot, meaning to crush the boy's skull beneath her heel, but a bedraggled, spitting devil flew at her face. Rumpledsilkskin burst from the weeds and climbed the flailing witch, clawing at her eyes. The wood witch teetered on one heel for an eternal second, and then crashed over backward. She fell like a demolished tower, but not before she had stepped squarely in the center of the magic ring.

AAIIEEEEEE! The witch keened and writhed, but the ring clamped about her ankle like a manacle. As the rain pelted them and the wind tore through the garden like a mad thing, a change overtook the creature the children had known as Nora. First she stiffened, and then she darkened to a brownish-grey. Her skin grew woody, her limbs contorted, her hair reached upward in a spray of slender tangled branches. Where her face had been was a long narrow hollow that looked disturbingly like a screaming mouth. The twisted black feet that had so upset Charles were indeed a spreading creep of roots. The transformation was swift; before their bewildered eyes lay a small, slender, thorny tree with a spectral blue ring around its roots.

Rumpledsilkskin sniffed at the toppled hawthorn tree and wrinkled her nose. Sorcery had such a smoldering stench. The rain sluiced down, settling in for a steady soaking. The wildness went out of the storm. The cat looked at the children standing in the downpour, their teeth chattering, and asked them to complete one more task.

"Drag her. To the rrring. The fairy rrring." She pranced in place, yowling the instructions over the steady percussion of the rain.

The tree was not large or heavy. A mere understory weed, really. Charles grasped it by the roots and tugged. The hawthorn slid with ease along the muddy ground. Adam and Amelia Rose joined him, and together they dragged the wood witch through the chilly rain to the bottom of the garden. There, the new gate opened without effort on its shiny hinges. On the other side of the narrow grassy verge, the Johns Woods bulked dark and silent. The rain penetrated the thick lacing of branches as a steady drip that was easy to mistake for footfalls. The wind picked its way here in breathy puffs and sighs. The trees creaked with ominous intent.

Just inside the penumbra of the trees, the fairy ring lay like a gay garland from happier times. The children dragged and rolled the hawthorn to its edge, the twisted branches slipping in their wet hands and the thorns scratching them spitefully. All three were bloodied by the time they managed to push the writhing roots across the lip of the ring. Ghostly blue light rose from the ring like fog and wrapped smoky tentacles around the hawthorn. There was a rending sound as the ground opened, and the little tree was eased upright, its roots *slurped* down into the humus. A shudder passed over its limbs, it emitted a low moan, and then it was still. It was rooted in the forest once again, this time for good.

Charles pushed his wet hair from his eyes, leaving a muddy streak on his brow. He was tired to his bones and empty of emotion. He looked at his siblings and thought that they looked older somehow. Not like the babies he had always thought them. There was grimness in Adam's eyes and a stoic bravery about Amelia Rose he had never seen before. He would have been surprised to see the steely expression on his own face had he a mirror.

The rain had slowed and the sky was brightening just a bit. Rumpledsilkskin was busily grooming her wet fur. From above him, deeper in the woods, Charles heard a bird begin to sing.

He put a hand on his brother's shoulder, gave a gentle tug on one of Amelia Rose's bedraggled curls. "Come on. Let's try to call Gram and Pop." He looked back at the brooding eaves of the house. "We can't stay here tonight."

"Will they come," Adam asked. Gram and Pop lived outside the city, nearly three hours away.

Charles's eyes were still on the house, gauging its level of awareness. Now that the witch was gone, maybe it would go back to sleep. He thought of the chewed shoe under the kitchen table and the fat red sofa like a bloated tick, and blinked back tears. No one would ever believe the house had eaten Mom and Dad; he wasn't sure he believed it himself.

"Yeah. They'll come. And we won't let them go inside."

In single file, the children made their way back through the garden to October House. Rumpledsilkskin stayed behind to sharpen her claws on the rough bark of the hawthorn tree.

Acknowledgements

There are many people to thank for the completion of this collection. I will start with the zany, talented members of Saturday Scribes, the writers' group that helped me to find my way to these stories and then encouraged me to tell them.

Thank you, Eleanor Curtis and Susan Keith, for being first readers and for volunteering several days and nights to assist with editing. You ladies rock!

Thank you, Tony Oliveri and Vikki Latta, for inspiring me and advising me.

Thanks to the Blogging Collective, fellow writers who returned again and again to read my tales and to cheer me on. Special thanks to writer Andra Watkins, who went out of her way to make sure folks knew my name.

Thanks to my grandma, Elma Felten, for investing in me and believing in me, no matter what crazy project I've got cooking.

And most of all, thanks to my husband and best friend, Jack. For being my rock and my haven, love always.

Made in the USA
Charleston, SC
22 May 2012